MW01037294

The Lady and the Mountain Doctor

The Mountain Series

Book 2

Misty M. Beller

ISBN: 0-9982087-3-6
ISBN-13: 978-0-9982087-3-2

Dedication

To my Mother.
For the love you show in every action, word, and prayer.
You are appreciated and loved more than you know.

Commit your way to the Lord,
Trust also in Him,
And He shall bring it to pass.

He shall bring forth your righteousness as the light,
And your justice as the noonday.

Rest in the Lord,
And wait patiently for Him.

Psalm 37:5-7a (NKJV)

Chapter One

October 28, 1876

Bryant Ranch - Near Butte City, Montana Territory

*M*iriam Bryant plunged her knife through the deer's thick winter fur, just the way her brother taught her. Crimson saturated the snow underneath, and she clenched her eyes tight against the sight. An acrid odor permeated the air. Miriam spun away, inhaling deep gulps of air.

They needed food. God sent the buck. She repeated the words in her head, as her stomach slowly unclenched. Finally, she turned back toward the animal, knife clutched tight in her hand. Once again, she wished she could have let the deer bound away in freedom. But their meat supply was low, and she had to pull her weight on the ranch.

The whisper of air was her only warning before a force slammed into her back, knocking her forward. A scream rent the air, and she writhed away from the creature pressing her against the deer carcass. *Cougar*. Pain pierced her body. Over and over. Everywhere the cat touched left new agony.

Miriam fought hard. She rolled onto her side and

tried to crawl, but the animal was all around her, growling and screaming. A blast of pain shot through her leg, and her body jerked hard. She reached for the source of the pain, and slammed her fists into the furry head, again and again.

Her vision grew fuzzy. Her fist no longer met fur. The pressure in her knee loosened, leaving behind a searing pain. She forced her elbows into the snow, dragging herself away from the animal. Clenching her teeth, she rolled over. Every inch of her frame screamed in torture, but she had to move in spite of the agony.

With her last ounces of strength, she rolled, pushing against the snow in one rotation after another. The freezing dampness of the icy flakes seeped under her coat, adding to the misery in her body.

Finally, her muscles wouldn't move anymore. The world spun around her, and then blackness closed in.

October 28, 1876
Butte City, Montana Territory

Alex Donaghue pressed hard on the mortar, grinding the root chunks against the wooden pestle. The Echinacea root had no scent, but tiny particles of powder drifted up to tickle his nose.

In the two months since he'd joined his brother, Bryan, at the clinic here in Butte, they'd run dangerously low on too many of their medicines. Demand from the hordes of miners in town far outweighed the random shipments of supplies they received. But that wasn't all bad, because it gave Alex the opportunity to get to know the flora in the area. It'd been a long time since he'd ground his own herbs, but it was a skill that came back easily.

The front door in the next room slammed open, admitting the noises from the muddy street outside.

"Help! Doc Bryan, you in here?"

Alex dropped the tools to the counter and strode toward the connecting doorway. He barely stopped himself from crashing into Gideon Bryant in the opening.

"Alex." Gideon's face was a mask of panic as he half-dragged Alex toward the open front door. "It's Miriam. She was attacked by a mountain lion. Blood everywhere. She's not wakin' up."

Stopping beside the wagon bed, Alex gripped the side and surveyed the scene. A blonde woman lay bundled in several blankets. Her eyes were closed, and her pale face streaked with blood and dirt. Leaves and twigs tangled in her golden hair. Reaching into the wagon, he rested his palm on her forehead. Warm, but not dangerously so. He held a finger to her upper lip. A faint tickle of air. Breathing, but not very strong.

In the wagon, Gideon gathered the blankets by her head in his fists. "Get the other end. We'll use the blanket like a stretcher."

Alex did as directed. He'd only met Gideon a few times, as his ranch was up the mountain a couple hours. Bryan knew him well, since Gideon and his wife Leah had been instrumental in setting up the clinic in this remote mining city. He'd heard of Gideon's sister Miriam, but not seen her until now. The grim look on Gideon's face showed his fear.

They carried her up the stairs, through the front office, and into the front examination room. "Easy does it."

They lowered her to the wood surface.

Alex eased the blankets open, starting at her neck and working toward her feet. Her buckskin coat was torn in several places. Shredded, really. But the main damage wasn't obvious until he uncovered her legs.

Blood everywhere. Is that why she hadn't regained consciousness? Her skirt gathered in a wad at her thigh, revealing a red-soaked petticoat and the left leg twisted in an irregular angle at the knee. Alex sucked in a breath.

"Bad?" Gideon's voice was flat, as if steeling himself for the worst.

Alex had been instructed in the art of the poker-face all four years at the McGill Faculty of Medicine. But this knee was painfully damaged. The lion had torn through her stocking and through the skin, revealing tendon, cartilage, ligament, and bone. This would take more than stitching the exterior layers together.

He looked up. "I'll need help with the surgery. Go get my brother. Should be at the Alice mine."

For a second, Gideon's eyes widened even more, darting between his sister and the window that overlooked the street. "All right." He strode toward the door, leaving Alex with a knot in his stomach, and a mountain of work ahead of him.

After cutting off the stocking, he inspected the rest of her. A few scratches that would need cleaning on her arm and calf, and deep puncture wounds on her back, but nothing that would require stitches. The position of the puncture wounds were high enough so they shouldn't have hit the lungs or other organs. But they were surely painful.

Focusing his attention on the knee, Alex cleaned the wound and prepared to examine the extent of the internal damage. A moan drifted from the woman, pulling his attention to her face. Her brows pulled together, creating deep furrows between them. Her eyes weren't open yet, but if the pain intensified from his efforts—which it surely would—that might bring her to full awareness. He moved to the cabinet and worktable to prepare the chloroform mask.

By the time boots sounded in the front room, Alex had inspected the wound in detail, and had a pretty good idea of what they'd need to do.

Male voices sounded through the wall, then Bryan entered the examination room alone. "What's going on with Little Sister?" He submerged his arms in the washbasin by the door as he listened to Alex's debriefing.

"It doesn't look like there's bone displacement or significant damage to the cartilage. The lateral collateral ligament has a second degree tear, but the worst seems to be a large tear in the patellar tendon. I think we'll need to stitch it before closing the wound and splinting."

"Do you have materials ready to repair the tendon?" Bryan settled a clean smock over his flannel shirt.

"Yes, but do you want to examine the damage first to confirm the diagnosis?"

Bryan raised a brow at him. "You already did that, didn't you?"

"Yes, but…" Why did it bother him that Bryan trusted his work?

His brother clapped him lightly on the back. "You take the lead and I'll assist."

Alex shrugged. "Let's get started then." After all, he'd spent the last nine years preparing to be a competent physician. What good was all that hard work if he didn't do what it took to save a life when the need arose?

Turning back to the patient, he positioned himself over her wounded knee. For just a second, he shot a glance at her pale face, loose blonde hair scattering across the table. It was almost his undoing.

Chapter Two

A lex snipped the silk thread over the feather quills along the incision in Miss Bryant's knee. There was consensus among his mentors at the McGill Faculty of Medicine that a quilled suture was right for stitching a wound this deep. He shot a glance at his brother from the corner of his eye. Did Bryan agree?

"Looks good." Bryan nodded, then gathered the forceps and other tools they'd used in the surgery.

Alex examined the wound again, trying to see it with fresh eyes. The sutures in the skin were clean. He'd stitched the delicate tendon fibers inside as well as he could, but most of the internal damage would have to heal on its own. Was that good enough? What if she sustained permanent damage that he could have corrected? He released a long breath. He'd done the best he could.

While Bryan washed the surgical instruments, Alex wrapped the wound with clean bandages, then fit the stiff leather splint over Miss Bryant's knee. Alex glanced at his brother when Bryan came to stand beside him. "Ready to remove the chloroform inhaler." He needed to prepare the laudanum for when she awoke. The pain was going to be rough for a while.

By the time Alex was satisfied with the placement and tightness of the splint, Bryan had already put away their equipment and removed his surgery smock.

"Gotta get back to the Alice if you don't need me. There was a small rockslide and I still have a few to tend." His big brother ran a hand through his amber brown hair. The color and loose curl was closer to their mother's, while Alex's hair was stick straight and dark brown like Pa's.

"I'll talk with Gideon. No problem. Thanks for the help." Alex hung his own smock on the hook beside Bryan's. Pausing, he glanced at his brother's retreating back. "Bryan?"

The familiar frame halted, then turned back to look at Alex.

"I think we should keep her here a week. At the clinic, I mean. Then make sure she stays nearby for a couple more?"

Bryan shrugged. "Your call. Sounds like a good plan."

A bit of tension left Alex's shoulders. Why did he always need Bryan's affirmation? It would get better the longer they worked together. Surely.

He followed Bryan through the doorway to the front room.

Gideon jumped to his feet the moment he saw them. "How is she?"

Alex stepped forward to address the man. "I think we accomplished what was needed in the surgery. She's still asleep, but should wake up soon. You can come back and see her if you'd like."

"Of course."

As Alex followed the man's long strides into the back room, he took in the broad shoulders and well-defined muscles. This mountain rancher wasn't a stranger to hard work.

Gideon hovered over his sister, her petite frame tiny in comparison to his.

Alex cleared his throat, then spoke in a low voice. "I'd like her to stay here at the clinic for at least a week. Her leg will require complete rest at first, then she'll need to start a few exercises. I'll want to keep an eye on the incision as well, and take the sutures out in two weeks." He eyed the taller man. Was he absorbing all the information?

The muscles in Gideon's jaw worked. "Whatever she needs."

"It'd be best if she could stay in town for at least a month or six weeks. We need to make sure the leg heals correctly and regains full motion."

Gideon's eyes shot to Alex's face. He didn't answer at first. Finally, he repeated his words. "Whatever she needs."

Relief washed through Alex as he released a breath. "Good." He motioned toward a chair by the wall. "Have a seat. Hard to say how long it'll take the chloroform to wear off."

Alex scanned the room. There wasn't really anything else he could do for the pair. But the mortar, pestle, and tiny chunks of Echinacea root still waited on the work counter for him to finish grinding.

While he worked, he kept an ear tuned to sounds behind him. All was quiet until Gideon spoke up. "What are you doing?"

Alex glanced back to see the man eyeing the mortar and pestle, a line furrowing his brow. "Grinding Echinacea root. Since we're heading into winter, I expect us to need a lot of this herb for colds and such."

"The medicine companies make you mix your own?"

A grin pulled Alex's face. "Local demand for a lot of remedies seems to be more than we can get with our irregular shipments. This country has good supply of some of the herbs, though. So I'll use what's available."

Before Gideon could respond, a groan from the table grabbed their attention. Miss Bryant's eyes flickered, then cracked enough to reveal a sliver of shadowed green. Her lips moved, but made no sound. The chloroform had likely turned her mouth to cotton.

Alex strode to the drinking pitcher and half-filled a tin cup. Slipping a hand behind the lady's shoulders, he eased her up just high enough so she could sip the water. "This should help. Only take a little, though."

She gulped twice, like a starved kitten finally given milk. Then she sank back as another moan slid from her lips.

"Let me get something for the pain." Setting the cup on the bedside table, he turned to get the tincture of laudanum he'd measured. Once again, he fitted his hand under her shoulders, careful to avoid the bandages on her back. "Here you go."

After swallowing, she sank against the thin pillow and her pale green eyes found his. "Thanks." The word seemed to take effort, and combined with the power of her gaze, formed a lump in his throat.

"You're welcome." His voice rasped, so he cleared it. Her gaze was so intense he couldn't hold it.

"Do you remember what happened, Miri?" Gideon's voice brought a welcome distraction.

Alex turned back to his worktable and plunged the mortar hard against the herb root in the pestle. His brain must still be strained from the surgery.

"I...was on my way home." Her voice was rough and the words came slowly. Was she having trouble remembering? They'd need to watch her for damage to the brain.

"There was a deer…a buck. I didn't want to bring him down, but I knew I should. I started to dress him…" Her words picked up speed, but stopped suddenly.

Alex stole a glance behind him. The delicate skin between her brows drew together.

Gideon patted her shoulder. "It's all right. I pretty much know what happened after that. Was on my way out when I heard your shot, then you screamed. If it makes you feel better, the mountain lion carcass is lying beside that buck you brought down."

Her face relaxed into the hint of a smile, although creases at the corners of her eyes signaled the pain she still felt. "At least there's something to show for this trouble. I'm sorry, Gideon. I didn't mean to put you through so much."

He huffed a dramatic sigh. "You always have been trouble."

"You're one to talk." She raised a brow.

Alex turned back to his worktable to hide his smile. How many times had he teased his younger sister, Cathleen, that way? And their middle sister, Brit, had been able to give it back better than he could dish it out. That is…before.

He ground harder on the mortar, pushing back thoughts of Brit. He needed to get this powder put away before dust contaminated it. Working in Dad's apothecary shop, he'd learned to protect the integrity of the herbs at all cost.

As Alex reached for an empty glass jar, he tried to tune out the conversation behind him. It wasn't hard, because Miss Bryant's voice had grown so soft he could barely make out the words. Probably the laudanum kicking in. And she did need to rest. Time to call an end to visiting hours.

He turned and leaned back against the work counter

to watch the scene. Gideon was telling her a story about a horse, but Miss Bryant's eyelids sagged. Every few seconds they would droop so low they concealed the green depths, then they'd pop back up to almost full mast. Only to repeat the process. The faint dusting of freckles across her nose and cheeks were like Cathleen's. But that's where the resemblance ended. Nothing else about this woman made him think of a sister.

In fact, very much the opposite.

Everything in Miriam wanted to give into the pull of oblivion. The pulsing in her leg had lessened a little. Enough so sleep had become the most important thing.

"I'll get a bite to eat while you sleep some."

She forced her eyes open again at Gideon's comment. He couldn't go yet, she still had questions. Focusing on forming her mouth into words, she pushed through the fog. "Will we go home tomorrow?"

Silence.

Gideon didn't answer, so she pushed her eyelids up again. Her brother and the doctor exchanged looks. What did that mean? The doctor took a step forward, bringing him into clearer focus. He was the younger brother she hadn't met yet.

"Miss Bryant, we had to repair a tendon in your knee. It should heal without problems, but I'd like to keep you under observation here at the clinic for at least a week to make sure there's no infection and no added strain."

A week? There was no way they could be gone from the ranch for half that long. Leah was there by herself even now, tending the stock and keeping the place running. And the first snow could hit any day. They still had so many things to do to prepare. But the doctor didn't stop talking long enough for her to set him straight.

"After that, I'd prefer you stay close to town for up to six weeks."

Miriam shook her head, but immediately stopped when pain shot through her temples. "I...can't." It would be so much easier to talk if her head would stop spinning.

"Miri, I'll go up and get Leah tomorrow, and we'll stay here in town with you." Gideon's voice had a soothing quality, like he was trying to keep her from getting riled. "John Stands-alone will keep an eye on the ranch for a few days. Then we'll see how you're healing."

Her temples started to hammer, making it so much harder to focus on her argument. "We need to go home tomorrow. I'll be fine." She closed her eyes against the pain pounding in her head.

"Sleep now, little sister. I'll come back in a couple hours and check on you." Gideon's warm, work-roughened hand brushed the hair off her forehead.

She forced her eyes open enough to attempt a smile. "Okay." Nothing could possibly be more important than sleep right now.

.

Chapter Three

*W*hen Miriam woke again, her eyelids still required great effort to raise. The sun streaming through the side window didn't help much, and a groan escaped as she turned away from the bright light.

"Hark. The sleeping lady stirs." The voice carried a lilting accent, but she couldn't wade through the fog in her mind to place its origin.

A figure came into view, and she blinked to clear her hazy vision. The doctor's brother. Or…he was a doctor, too. But he was the new one. Smiling brown eyes shimmered under a thick layer of brown hair scattered across his forehead, giving him a playful look.

"And how feel ye today, m'lady? In need of a helpful remedy?"

She blinked again. His accent sounded like Leah's stories of the Knights of the Round Table in Camelot. Where was she?

A grin pulled at one side of his mouth. "In other words, are you in pain this morning?" His voice lost the accent, slipping into a rich tenor. "I can give you something to take the edge off if you need it."

Miriam carefully tightened her muscles, taking stock of what hurt.

Everything.

When she tried to shift her legs, the left one screamed in pain. Her upper back throbbed, and everything else just plain ached. She stopped moving and clamped her teeth against a whimper. She would not look like a weak child in front of this man, practically a stranger. And a physician from a big eastern city, at that.

Shifting her focus to the doctor, she found him watching. Sadness lined the corners of his eyes. When he caught her gaze, his dark brows rose, a pleasant expression lighting his face again. "Shall we start with tea? Mum always said a good cup of tea could cure a world of ills."

"Yes, thanks."

He was already striding toward something behind her. Dishes clanged, then he appeared a minute later with a tin cup, steam wafting from its brim. Miriam reached for it, but her position was awkward, lying flat on the bed.

"Let's get you settled." The doctor placed the cup on a table by the wall, then reached for a thick folded quilt. "I'm going to raise you up a bit."

Miriam tried to help as he lifted her shoulders, pillow and all. Every limb in her body moaned against the effort.

"Easy there. Just let me do the work. You can lay back now." He crooned the words, a bit of the earlier accent lacing his voice again. The rhythmic cadence and tenor of his voice was so calming, soothing the tension in her muscles as she followed his direction. Not to mention the warmth of his hand on her shoulder, even through her sleeve.

"There now. Is that a little better?" He stepped back and scanned her from head to toe.

Even though she was covered to her shoulders by a

thick wool blanket, heat crawled up Miriam's neck. What must she look like in front of this stranger? Her hair tickled her cheeks, apparently escaped from the braid she usually wore. Her hand itched to smooth the strays, but that would be too obvious.

The doctor turned to a small side table and carried it to the middle of the room beside her bed. "We'll move you to the spare sickroom later today. You'll have a little more privacy there." He raised his head to meet her gaze with a wink. "And the bed is immeasurably more comfortable than this rock-solid examination table."

What was it about this man that made her want to smile? Just hearing him talk lifted her spirits, pushing away everything that weighed her down.

He brought the tin cup again, and placed it in her hands. "It's probably cooled enough." Their fingers brushed in the transfer, raising bumps along the surface of her arms.

"Thank you." She mumbled the words, her gaze dropping to the amber liquid. It was almost a relief that it took all her focus to keep her hands from shaking as she raised the drink to her mouth. Was she so weak from the accident? Or was the trembling merely from being close to this man? She needed to clear that thought from her head pronto. He was a doctor, here to cure the sick and injured residents of the territory.

She was just another patient among the throngs.

A door opened in another room, and boot thumps sounded on the wood floor. The doctor strode to the doorway. "Gideon. She woke just a few minutes ago."

Her brother followed the doctor into the room, taking her measure in one swift gaze. "How you feelin' today?" He grabbed a wooden chair from beside the desk and settled next to her bed.

"All right, I guess." She forced her lips to form a reassuring smile.

One of his brows arched. "Pretty lousy, huh?"

This time the smile came easier. "Like I was attacked by a mountain lion."

He nodded, then looked up at the man working at the stove in the corner. "Doc Alex takin' good care of you?"

Miriam's gaze drifted to the man. Alex. It fit him— with the Irish brogue he slipped into so easily.

At Gideon's words, the man—Doc Alex—turned and sent her another wink. That simple motion produced a flurry in Miriam's midsection, clearing her head of all thought. What had the question been? She glanced up at Gideon. That's right, the doctor's care. The feeling of Alex's hands brushing hers as he gave her the warm tea flashed through her mind. She'd better not let that emotion show. "Yes, he's been a good doctor."

Gideon nodded. "I'm sure you feel better after sleeping so long." He must not suspect her of any improper feelings. That was a man for you. Couldn't see emotion if it smacked 'em in the nose.

"Doc, you still think she needs to stay a week?" Gideon addressed his question to the doctor, who turned from the stove to study them.

"Yes, at least. It's critical for her leg not to be strained these first few days. If she pushes too hard, it could permanently damage the knee."

Gideon's deep green eyes turned to her, and he leaned forward to rest his elbows on his knees. "Miri, I need to go up the mountain and get Leah. She'll be worried sick if I stay away any longer. But we'll be back tomorrow."

Miriam's chest squeezed at the anguish in her brother's face. He'd lost so many people he loved. But she wasn't about to be counted among them. Placing a hand on his clasped fingers, she squeezed reassurance. "I'll be fine, big brother. Stay at the ranch a few days and get things ready for winter. You heard the doctor. I can't do anything but sit here for a week. Come back to get me then."

He pulled back, brows lifting. Obviously, her response wasn't what he expected. "That's a far cry from what you said last night."

Last night? What had she said? Something tickled the corners of her mind. Something about arguing with Gideon and the doctor. But what had she argued about? Ugh. Thinking so hard made her head ache. No matter. She tightened her jaw, giving Gideon her no-nonsense look. "I don't know what I said last night, but this is what I want. Go home to Leah, take care of the ranch, and come back for me in a week."

His gaze scanned her face, then raised to the doctor standing by the window. "I don't know, Doc. What do you think?"

Doc Alex came to stand at the foot of her bed. "She'll be well cared for, Gideon." His voice slipped back into the Irish brogue as a twinkle flashed in his eye. "We'll serve her tea in china cups and play whist and dominos."

Gideon raised a single brow at the man. "That should be interesting." He leaned back in his chair, eyeing Miriam through narrow slits. "All right. Anything you need before I head up the mountain?"

Miriam scanned the blanket covering her lower half. She still wore the blue wool dress from when she was attacked. Could she stand the same clothes for a week? But if she sent Gideon to the store for ready-made clothes, who knew what he'd come back with? No. She could make do with this dress until Leah came. But what about underthings? No way was she going to have Gideon buy any ready-made.

Her gaze flickered to Gideon's, then skittered around the room. He might be capable of purchasing the fabric and thread. Could she cut the material and sew new drawers while she stayed in bed? She nibbled her bottom lip. It might be worth trying.

She looked back to her brother. "Could you pick up a few things from the Dry Goods? I'll write them down if you have paper and charcoal."

"There's a sheet for you right here." The doctor strode toward the little writing desk by the door, then handed her a paper and pencil nub.

Within minutes, Gideon and her list left, and Doc Alex settled a tray across her lap. Steam wafted from some kind of yellow gruel on the plate in the center. Her gaze lifted to find him standing a few feet away, eyeing her.

His mouth quirked as he met her look. "It's not quite tea and crumpets, but I was low on supplies."

With that charming, slightly roguish grin on his face, he could have served her pig slop, and she wouldn't have much to complain about. Miriam dropped her focus to the food, took up a spoonful of gruel, and raised it to her mouth. It tasted a little better than it looked. Heavy on the cornmeal, but not too dry.

The doctor placed her refilled mug on the table beside her, then settled into the chair Gideon had vacated. He held his own steaming tin cup in both hands. Was he going to watch her eat? Suddenly, the room seemed unseasonably hot. She kept her focus on the yellow mixture, and raised another spoonful to her mouth.

"So tell me, Miss Bryant. What does a lady like yourself do in your leisure time?"

A lady? Miriam's head jerked up as she stared at him. No one had ever called her a lady. Not up on the mountain. Not wearing a dirty homemade wool dress with her hair falling halfway out of her braid.

"Do you play dominos? Write letters? Tame mountain lions?" That dimple pressed into his cheek again.

A nervous titter escaped Miriam before she could stop it. Leisure? "Umm... Leah and I like to read together. It works, because one of us can still get things done while the other reads."

A sparkle lit his eyes. "Really? What do you read?"

She nibbled another spoonful before answering. "Anything, really. Leah brought a whole trunk full of books when she first came to the ranch. Charles Dickens, Louisa May Alcott, even some thrilling sea novels by Herman Melville. Have you heard of him?"

"*Typee*, and *Moby Dick*?"

A smile tugged at Miriam's mouth, despite the throbbing in her leg. "Yes. Leah calls them heavy reading, but to me they're fascinating. Can you imagine traveling all the places he's been? I've always dreamed of seeing foreign lands and exotic animals."

His brows rose just a bit, and he leaned back. Was that respect shining in his gaze? "You'd like to be a sailor on a whaling ship?"

Heat crawled up her back. "I might rather ride in first class with a traveling companion or two."

That twinkle sparked in his amber eyes again, and his voice slipped into the brogue. "Ah... I knew ye were a lady from the moment I set me eyes on ye, didn't I now."

A twinge of pain shot from her knee up into her hip, but Miriam tried not to wince. She was enjoying this conversation too much to be put off by her injuries. "So what of you, Doctor Donaghue?" She couldn't quite bring herself to call him Doc Alex to his face, even though Gideon had done it. "Have you traveled the world? Maybe studied medicine in England?"

"Please, call me Alex. Doctor Donaghue is my big brother."

Miriam paused. Would that be appropriate? Titles were pretty informal in the Territory, with most men going by nicknames alone. Slim, or Stubby, or Gimp. But Leah had been teaching her the etiquette of a lady, in preparation for their big trip East next summer. And Leah said a lady never addresses a man by his first name. Still...he was asking her to. Wouldn't it be impolite to refuse?

She took a deep breath. "Okay. So...Alex, have you traveled abroad?" His name was magical rolling across her tongue. Would he think she was crazy if she said it again?

He shrugged, his chin dipping in a self-conscious expression. "I was raised in Boston, studied medicine in Montreal, and now I've finally made it to Butte City." He spread his hands as if this dirty mining town were the mecca of all he'd aspired to.

Montreal? Wasn't that in Canada? She opened her mouth to ask, but pain shot through her leg again. This time it was much more than a twinge. More like a bullet. She bit her lip against a cry.

Alex sprang forward, removing the tray from her lap. "Is it your knee? I'll ready another dose to help with the pain."

Miriam nodded. The ache in her knee had radiated through her leg now, and wasn't subsiding. *Lord, help me.* It seemed to take forever, but Alex finally reappeared by her side with a tincture of thick brownish liquid.

"Thanks." She could barely push the word out as

more than a whisper. Her fingers shook as she raised the container to her lips and drained it.

"Sleep now if you can." Alex's voice was soothing, almost like a lullaby. "Would you like another cup of willow tea?"

Miriam shook her head, but then stopped as pain ricocheted through her temples. "No, thanks."

A hand stroked the hair from her forehead. Gentle, yet strong. Or maybe she imagined it.

Chapter Four

Alex tore his gaze from the woman sleeping in the center of the room. She was so beautiful, in a half-wild, half-elegant sort of way. But she was a patient. Those thoughts shouldn't enter his mind. Gripping the edges of the crate, he lifted it slowly so the clink of medicine bottles didn't wake his patient. After slipping out the door, he pulled it shut behind him.

She slept in their primary examination room, so he'd made do with seeing patients in the spare room all day. Unfortunately, the medicines and instruments he typically used were all stocked in the room where she napped peacefully. When Bryan came back that afternoon, they'd have to see about moving her.

The sound of the front door opening drifted down the hall, followed by a wet, hacking cough. He settled the crate on the work counter in the empty room, then strode toward the front waiting area.

"How can I help you?" He inserted a genial tone into his voice as he spoke to the two men. One leaned heavily on the other. His slender limbs looked barely strong enough to hold him up.

"M'brother's in a bad way." The stronger man eyed him, his bushy black beard matching the dark hair that stuck out in several directions. The other man must be the older brother, maybe close to a decade older, as his brown hair was evenly streaked with salty gray. Or maybe the illness had aged him prematurely.

"Come on back." Alex waved for them to follow him and made his way toward the empty examination chamber.

Coughing echoed down the hall as the men obeyed his direction. Deep hacks that signaled moisture in the lungs. Alex helped the man lower himself to sit on the bed. "I'll need you to unfasten the top five buttons on your shirt."

The man seemed too exhausted to do more than slowly comply, while his dark-haired brother paced near the door.

Alex picked up his Cammann's stethoscope from the table and slipped the ivory earpieces into his ears. "Can you take some deep breaths in and out?" With the bell-shaped piece settled over the man's lungs, Alex squinted as he listened. A gurgling noise accompanied the rush of air.

After checking several other operations of the patient's lungs, as well as other body functions, concern weighed Alex's own chest. The man could scarcely breathe. But Alex needed a better understanding of his lifestyle before he could properly diagnose the cause.

He turned away from the patient to pour a dose of elecampane. "Tell me, Mr. Langley, which mine do you work in?"

"The Parrott." The younger brother barked the words.

Alex favored the burly man with only a glance, then focused again on the dosing cup in his hand. He carried it to the older brother, who'd given his name as Mick Langley, and helped the frail man raise it to his mouth. "This should help your breathing right away."

After swallowing the dose, Langley slumped over his knees. As if the simple act of drinking had worn him out. How did he work fourteen hour days digging through rock in a mine shaft?

Alex pulled a chair to face the bed and settled into it, his hands on his legs. He needed some answers, but the man had to be put at ease first. Good time to bring out the ol' Irish accent. "Sorry you're not feelin' well, lad. Can you tell me when it first came on?"

Langley raised filmy eyes to stare at him. "Been years."

Alex's brows rose before he could stop them, but he tried to keep his tone gentle. "An' you're just now comin' to see me?"

The younger man, Tad, stepped forward, as if protecting his brother from the censure in Alex's words. "Doc Bryan give 'im a treatment at the mine a few times. The coughin' didn't get bad 'til last week. You got more o' that stuff the other doc give 'im?"

Alex turned his focus to Tad. The man obviously wanted to feel like he was doing something for his big brother. "It was most likely the elecampane I just administered. I need a little more information so I can prescribe a treatment plan."

He looked back at Mick, and fought the desire to hold the man upright, lest he collapse onto the floor. "Would you like to lay down, Mick?"

His bleary eyes turned to blink at the pillow beside him. "Naw. Harder to breathe when I'm lay—" Another thick, chesty cough broke off his words.

That old, helpless feeling settled over Alex as he watched his patient struggle. Was there something else he should be doing? He would prescribe a steam bath and licorice chews. And the man needed to get away from the mines, with their stifling heat and lack of quality air to breathe. Rest would likely do more for him than most medicines.

When the coughing fit subsided, Alex leaned forward, elbows on his knees, giving Mick his most earnest and caring expression. "I need to understand what a normal day is like for you, Mick, so I can find what's making you sick. Can you start by telling me where you live?"

"A shanty outside of town. Near the mines." Tad spoke for his brother again.

Alex glanced up at him. "Do the two of you live together?"

"With a couple other blokes."

Four men living in a shack. He'd seen some of those structures, usually a single room, with a stove in the corner and bedrolls on the floor. The boards spanning the walls often left cracks wide enough for ice pellets to blow in during a hailstorm. Not the kind of place for a patient with sick lungs to heal in the middle of winter.

Another coughing fit seized Mick, adding an additional layer of helplessness on Alex's shoulders. But he shook it off. He'd help this man if it took every breath in his body.

Turning to the younger brother, Alex leveled his voice. "I'd like him to stay here in the clinic for a few days. He needs rest and regular care."

"No." Mick grabbed Alex's arm, even as he fought off another cough. "Haf...ta...work."

"You'll die in that mine if you don't take a break." Alex fought the anger rising in his chest. "You have to rest, Mick. And give your body a chance to heal. I can work with you here and try different remedies. We'll find what works for you, then you can keep doing it at home. You'll not get better, though, if you run yourself into the ground."

Mick raised his head in a long, painful movement, and met Alex's gaze with his milky stare. "If I don't work, I'll lose my job. Then I'll just be a burden. Gonna go some time or other. Might as well earn my keep 'til then."

Alex's heart plummeted to his toes. Was that truly his outlook? *Gonna die anyway?* What could he say to make this man accept help?

Tad stepped closer. "Just give us the medicine, doc. I'll be takin' care of my brother. You tell me what he needs, an' I'll see to it."

Mick was already struggling to stand, and Tad reached to help him.

Alex released a sigh. "All right. I'll give you instructions and herbs to take with you. Come back tomorrow and we'll see how you're progressing."

Minutes later, Alex watched the men trudge down the hall toward the front door. Mick leaned heavily on his brother. There was no way the man could work at the mine in his condition. Hopefully, one of the treatments he'd prescribed would help.

And what was causing the fluid and weakness in his lungs? Tuberculosis? Pneumonia? Either one could kill the man if left untended. He may be too far gone, even now, for anything to be successful. But what if there was something Alex missed?

Releasing a long breath, he turned toward the room where Miss Bryant slept. He cracked the door quietly, but she turned to face the movement. Forcing a cheery smile, he stepped inside. "You slept through lunch, but you're in luck."

"Luck?" Her voice was thick with sleep, and the spray of honey-blonde curls that spread across her pillow made his fingers itch to touch them. Not a good response.

He strode to the pot-bellied stove in the corner. "Yes. I saved you a dish of Irish stew. And you've not lived until you've tasted an Irishman's stew." He stepped backward so she could see his face, and sent her a cock-eyed grin. "Unfortunately, Mum only taught Bryan the proper technique, so mine's not half as good."

The smallest hint of a smile touched her lips, spreading warmth through his chest. That smile was worth working for. He ladled the soup into a cup, scrunching his nose at the thick, stickiness of the mixture. Must've sat on the stove too long.

He placed the mug in Miss Bryant's hands. "It's not the best I've ever served."

She examined the brew, raising her spoon and watching the viscous liquid slowly drip from the utensil. Heat crept up his neck.

"I'm sure it's tasty." Her mouth curved, but no sparkle lit her eyes. Lines at the corners spoke of the pain she must still feel.

A bit of willow tea might help. He marched back to the stove and pulled the jar of willow bark from the shelf. "How's your injury feeling?"

There was a pause before she spoke. "Better."

That was a falsehood if he'd ever heard one. He filled a mug with steaming water from the kettle on the stove, then stirred leaves into it. "Better than a needle prick when you're sewing? Or better than if your knee were still torn open?"

"The latter, I guess."

He traded Miss Bryant the steaming cup of tea for the mug of overcooked soup, and her eyes wandered up to meet his. They were the prettiest shade of clear green, nicely accented by the pink now tinging her cheeks. Her gaze dropped to the liquid swirling in the cup.

He should step back, give her room. Not make her uncomfortable. But something kept him rooted, right there in front of her. After setting the stew on the side table, his hands found the pockets of his gray wool pants. What should he say? The silence lingered thick between them.

"When Bryan comes back tonight, we'll move you to the softer bed in the other room. We need to change your bandages, too."

She nodded, her gaze not meeting his. "All right."

"You might be able to rest better there, too. It's part of the old structure, so sound doesn't carry as easy through those walls."

No answer, but she'd just about finished off the tea. He should get back to work, and let her rest in peace. A pile of correspondence awaited him. He also needed to make case notes on the last several patients and update their inventory. So why didn't he turn and walk away?

At last, she raised those green eyes to him. "Thank you."

This was why he couldn't bring himself to leave the room. Her look was magical. Drawing him in.

A smile pushed onto his face, as he took the empty cup from her. "You're welcome. Anything else you need?"

She hesitated, nibbled her lip, and glanced at her knee.

He wavered. Should he give her another dose of laudanum? She was obviously in pain, but the last thing she needed was to become dependent on the medicine. The least he could do was share his concerns. "It's time you can have another dose of medicine, but only if you need it. The laudanum has addictive qualities, so we should be careful with it."

Her eyes grew wide. "I'll just sleep then." She was so strong and brave. Not once had she complained, even though the pain must be terrible.

"Okay, but I'll be in the other room. If you change your mind or need anything, call." He brushed a strand of hair from her shoulder. It was an automatic gesture, and he didn't realize what he was doing until his skin registered the softness of the curl. He fought the urge to sink his fingers into the rest of it.

He spun away from her and strode toward the door. What was he doing? He'd better get a handle on himself quick. And not come back into this room until he did.

It was over an hour later before he trusted himself to check on Miriam again. When he eased the door open, her eyes were closed, and the blanket rose and fell in a steady movement. The pain lines around her eyes were still there, but a little softer in sleep.

His gaze wandered down to where the wool fabric covered her knee. Did he do everything he could during the surgery? Had he done it right? What if the leg became infected? He'd find out tonight when they changed the bandage. But even if the incision healed cleanly, what if she never regained the motion in her knee? What if he'd ruined her chances of a normal life?

Alex pulled the door closed, but couldn't shut out the questions. Could he live with himself if he destroyed this beautiful woman?

Chapter Five

"You worked late tonight." Alex handed his brother a mug of coffee. They stood in the main room of their living quarters, just off the clinic.

Bryan sighed, closing his eyes as he sipped the brew. "Stopped at Wallace's to see if we had any shipments."

"Did we?"

"Nothing." Bryan released another long breath. "We're running short on several tonics and herbs. Especially elecampane."

Alex's forehead tightened. "I had a couple miners in here today. Mick and Tad Langley. Mick's lungs are pretty bad off. Said he's seen you a couple times at the Parrott."

Bryan's brows pinched. "Yeah. Sounded like he had fluid in his lungs, or pneumonia maybe. Told him to come in here if it didn't get better."

Alex sank into the ladder-back chair by the door to the clinic. "I tried to get him to board at the clinic a few days. He lives in one of the hovels near the mines, and I know that's only making it worse. He wouldn't stay, though. Said he'd rather die working, than take a break and be a burden to his brother." Scrubbing a hand through his hair, Alex looked up at his big brother. "I don't know if what I prescribed will be enough to save him."

Bryan pulled off his thick wool coat. "What did you give him?"

As Alex relayed the medicines and directions he'd recommended, Bryan nodded at each one. "There's not anything else I can think of. Sounds like you covered every angle."

Despite the reassurance, a weight still pressed on Alex's shoulders. "Do you think there's something we're missing here? Is it conditions at the mines causing all the breathing complaints? Or do you think it's the primitive living quarters? It's barely November and already as cold as it ever got in Montreal. Some of these cabins are sparse enough to let the wind blow through them. How could the men not take sick?"

Bryan took up his coffee cup from the table and clapped Alex on the shoulder. "We'll work on it, but we're not gonna fix the whole thing tonight. Is there dinner on the stove?"

Alex slowly rose to his feet and followed his brother down the clinic hall to the main exam room. The room held the cook stove, so that's where most of the food preparation and eating was done. He lowered his voice as they drew near the closed door. "I told Miss Bryant we'd move her to the other chamber this evening so she's not disturbed as much. We'll need to check her incision, too."

"All right."

Bryan was the first through the doorway, and Miss Bryant's voice was stronger than earlier as she greeted him. "Doc Bryan."

Her smile was genuine, and even reached her eyes. Alex's stomach clenched. What he wouldn't give for that smile to be turned on him.

"I hear you're ready to move to better quarters, Miss Miriam. Mind if we take a look at the bandages first?"

She shifted the blankets around her leg to reveal the leather splint they'd put over the cotton strips. "Of course."

Bryan took the lead in the examination, much to Alex's relief. Could he have completely separated his personal feelings from his medical role? He'd always thought he could. That had never been an issue for the four years at medical school and during his internship. But there was something bewitching about this woman.

Bryan seemed pleased with the progress. He asked Miss Bryant several questions about her level of pain, and if she'd had any trouble with the minimal activity required to use the chamber pot. Of course, her cheeks turned that pretty pink when she answered that she was managing. Alex forced himself not to stare.

"Well, then. Looks like we're ready to move you." Bryan turned to Alex. "Is the other room ready?"

"Clean and fresh blankets on the bed."

"Good. I think the best way is for one of us to carry her, and the other support the injured leg."

Somehow, Alex ended up with one arm under Miss Bryant's shoulders, and the other supporting her legs. Her hands clasped his neck, holding her close. The warmth of her breath fanned his neck. Even through layers of clothes, every place she touched began to tingle. She was light as he cradled her. So vulnerable, the desire to protect her welled up in his chest. He would do everything in his power to care for this woman, and restore her to complete health.

Miriam forced her eyes open, fighting against the pounding in her head. She blinked, pushing sleep aside, but the banging didn't stop. It wasn't in her head. Well, not completely. Aside from the pain that still pulsed through her, someone was beating on a door down the hall. What was happening?

She glanced first to the window, where faint daylight filtered over the street outside, then to the open door to the hall. Steps sounded in the hallway, with a strange rhythm. *Clump, thud, clump, thud.* The reason became obvious when Doc Bryan hobbled by. One boot on and the other clutched in his hand. During the quick glimpse as he rushed by, she captured an image of his auburn hair wet and curling across his forehead. Suspenders hooked over his bare shoulders. Someone must have a terrible need for the doctor.

"I'm coming. Don't knock the wall down." His words didn't seem to make an impact, because the pounding kept on.

A man's voice yelled from outside. The sound of wood scraping drifted down the hall, then the door opening.

"Donaghue!" The male voice blasted from the front room. It was followed by the murmur of Doc Bryan's voice, although she couldn't make out his words.

"Where's that lousy, slow-witted brother of your'n?" The voice rose even louder, ignoring Doc Bryan's muffled attempts to calm him. "Let me at him!"

Miriam pushed herself to a sitting position. What had the man so riled? And why in England would he have something against Alex?

34

More footsteps sounded, but not as loud as Bryan's. Alex strode past her doorway, his face a stoic mask.

"Alex," she whispered. But he didn't hear.

The commotion in the front room was growing, and even Bryan's voice was now loud enough to be perfectly understood. "Your brother was sick, Tad. Doc Alex did everything possible."

"He poisoned him. That potion he gave put Mick over the edge. My brother would still be alive if it weren't for that sorry son-of-a—."

"Langley!" Bryan's voice bit the air so sharply, the whole clinic came to a hush.

Then another noise came. The sound of…crying? Yes, sobs. Manly weeping.

Miriam's heart squeezed. She knew what it was like to lose a brother. When Abel, her middle brother, was mauled by the bear, she thought her chest would split open inside. She cried for months, any time the memories struck. It was only Leah's coming that really pulled her out of the pit of grief.

A need sprung up inside her. She had to go to the men. There may not be much she could do, but maybe she'd find something. Pushing the blanket aside, she placed her good right leg on the floor. Then with her hands, she lowered her left leg, biting her lip against the pain stabbing her knee. Bracing both hands on the work table by the wall, she scooted sideways on her right leg, dragging her bad leg behind her. It took forever, but she finally made it around the edge of the room to the doorway. Her breath came heavy. Who would have thought it was so much work to hobble such a short distance?

Clutching the door frame for support, she looked down the long hallway to the front room. Alex stood motionless at the end of the corridor, feet braced, and hands clenched at his sides. The light was in front of him, so she couldn't make out his face until he turned to the side.

The stricken look there took her breath away.

Alex's muscles wouldn't move.

Mick Langley died? The patient he'd treated not two days ago. Was Tad right? Had the medicine Alex prescribed killed him? *Oh, God. No!*

He wanted to sink to his knees there on the wood floor. But his legs were frozen stiff. Had he killed another patient? From his ineptitude? His fists clenched tighter.

"Mick was a sick man, Tad. I pray he's in a better place now." Bryan held the grieving brother at arm's length, while the man wiped his eyes on a grimy sleeve.

"Mama always prayed her boys'd go to heaven." Tad's voice cracked.

"Do you want me to come back to the house with you?"

Tad shook his head, gaze dipping to his boots. "Naw. The boys're already diggin' a grave."

A memory flashed through Alex's mind of another fresh mound of dirt. With white posies planted at the head. He clenched his eyes tight against the image.

"I'll stop by later today, then." Bryan turned the man, and kept his arm around the fellow's shoulders as they shuffled toward the door. "Is there anything I can bring you?"

The room grew foggy around Alex, and the voices faded away. A memory pulled at him. He was sitting beside

Britt's lifeless body. Her little eyelids closed, hand limp between his. Tears streamed down his face as he cried her name, over and over. But she never answered.

He hadn't meant to hurt her. Hadn't meant for her to follow him on his deliveries. If only he'd slowed down when he saw her. Not made her run beside him. He knew she had the breathing episodes. Knew it wasn't good for her to run. But he'd not been thinking about her. Only himself. And how much he wanted to get home and play ball with Bryan's friends. Poor Britt. Why had she idolized a stupid lout like him? She'd deserved a brother who cared. Not someone whose selfish neglect killed her.

"Alex."

He turned away from the voice that threatened to pull him from the memories.

"Alex." A firm hand pressed his shoulder, giving it a slight shake.

He blinked, staring into Bryan's face.

"It wasn't your fault, Alex."

He swallowed to bring moisture back into his mouth. "Yes. It was." He barely recognized his own voice, the way it rasped.

"Langley was in bad shape the last time I saw him. You said yourself he may not make it living in that drafty shack."

Alex squinted at his brother. Langley? What about Britt? And then the last of the fog cleared. His patient, Mick Langley. Another wave of sorrow crashed over him. "What did I do wrong, Bry?" He searched his brother's brown eyes for the answer.

"There wasn't anything else you could do. His chances would have been better if he'd stayed here under our care, but you can't force a man." Bryan ran a hand through his damp hair. "It's a hard life for these miners. Most of 'em die early. All we can do is help the ones we can. For the rest, make 'em as comfortable as possible until the end. You did your job, brother."

Bryan pulled him close and mussed the back of Alex's hair, the way he used to when Alex was a boy. The gesture felt odd, now that they were almost the same height, but the familiarity soothed the inflamed edges of Alex's nerves. Bryan slipped his arm around Alex's shoulders, and together they walked down the hallway to their quarters. It was the same way Bryan had walked the miner to the front door. His older brother had a soothing manner that made you feel things would be okay. Tomorrow would be another day.

But when tomorrow came, could he do a better job than he'd done today?

Chapter Six

*F*our days in bed. It was mid-morning the next day, and Miriam flipped through yet another boring medical text. What she really wanted to do was toss the book aside and run outside screaming.

Her leg was healing. At least it had stopped the constant throbbing, so it didn't hurt as much to be awake. But she was still practically tied to this bed. The only exercise she'd been allowed was pulling the chamber pot from beneath her bed. Just the few actions required for that still sent fire through her knee, though.

She'd finished stitching an extra pair of drawers from the material Gideon purchased before he left town. Now there wasn't much else to do except read boring medical books and stare out the window at the gray sky and occasional wagon passing. The mountain peaks in the distance seemed to taunt her. She bit down a growl. How many more days would she be locked in this tiny chamber?

Turning the next page, she skimmed the text. Her stomach clenched and she wrinkled her nose at a sketch of a thin snake-like animal, then flipped the page again. It was morbidly interesting to read about using leeches to bleed people. But she'd already examined as much as she could stomach.

Alex had been kind to bring her the books, even if they were as interesting as dirty dish water. He'd shrugged and, with his neck turning red, said these were all the books they had. And then he'd slipped into that Irish accent and said something about too bad Bryan was such a boring chap.

A smile tugged at Miriam's mouth. Seemed every memory of Alex brought a smile. He was so much fun to talk to, with an easy manner that made patients relax and enjoy his company. So different from his brother. Bryan seemed more quiet and reserved. Kind of like her own brother, Gideon. She'd never understood why Gideon didn't speak his mind. But, of course, she loved him anyway.

As if her thoughts summoned him, Doc Bryan's voice hummed in the hallway outside her door as he led a patient to the examination room beside her chamber. That morning, he'd announced he'd be staying at the clinic today, and Alex was to take the day off.

Naturally, Alex had argued. But not as much as she would have expected. He'd been so quiet since the episode with Tad Langley the day before. Poor Alex. He cared deeply about his patients, and losing the elder Mr. Langley had hit him hard. She tried to get him to talk, but he seemed buried deep in another time and place. Like he was merely going through the motions here in the clinic. Hopefully, time away would help.

A thump sounded through the walls, as someone slammed the front door. Miriam flipped the book closed and placed it on the bedside table, then eased back against the pillows and closed her eyes. She could dream about the trip she and Leah planned for the summer.

A few days in St. Louis, then on to Richmond where Leah had grown up. Leah had talked for days about her eagerness to see Emily, her former companion. After hearing so much about the woman, Miriam's excitement had bubbled up, too. It wasn't confirmed yet, but Leah had asked Emily to accompany them up to Philadelphia, New York, and Boston.

Hadn't Alex said he and Bryan were from Boston? Maybe she could visit his family while there. Pass along any messages. See the place they'd grown up. The corners of her mouth tugged. It'd be interesting to learn more about what had formed these two talented brothers.

"Be ye hungry, m'lady?"

Miriam's heart thumped faster as her eyes flew open. Alex grinned from the doorway. She swallowed. "I...um..."

Her gaze dropped to the wooden tray he held with both hands. A white cloth covered whatever it held.

As he stepped into the room, her hand wandered up to her hair. What she wouldn't do for a bath. Or at least a clean dress. And her hair must look like a bird's nest. Curls kept slipping out of her braid, and she hadn't taken time to redo the plat that morning.

"Here ye are, miss." Alex placed the tray on the bed next to her, and Miriam scooted over to allow more room. "A meal fit for the bonniest lass in the county." With a flourish, he swiped the cloth covering.

Miriam drew in a breath, and a faint spicy aroma tickled her nose. "It's beautiful, Alex." A delicate china plate with pink roses painted around the edge held sandwich quarters. Steam wafted from the matching teacup, its fluted handle in the form of a rose leaf.

"Only the finest for the fair lady who graces us with

her presence." He stepped back and bowed, performing the motion as if gracing Queen Victoria herself. Then he glanced up, his mouth tilting in an off-kilter grin. "And if you're a good girl and clean your plate, there may be a surprise in it for you."

Miriam bit back a smile, but it escaped anyway. "Oh, really?"

She scanned the tray again, with its delicate place setting. But there was only enough for one. "Where's yours?" Her gaze found his, which turned sheepish.

His hands slipped into his pockets, and his right foot scuffed the floor. "I...uh. The smell was too much for me, I'm afraid. Ate my sandwich on the way over."

A giggle bubbled inside her. "I suppose that shouldn't surprise me. I had brothers, too. Won't you at least take tea with me?"

He shrugged and pulled up a chair. "No tea, but I'll sit and visit awhile."

Miriam almost regretted her offer, as his gaze settled on her. She was in no condition to be the center of attention, especially from this very attractive man. His eyes tracked her hand as she reached for a sandwich. She needed to start a conversation, but what to say?

"This china is so pretty. Is it yours?"

His chuckle sent heat up her neck. Had she really just asked a man if he owned china?

"No, from the café. Aunt Pearl's finest. I had to promise a year's worth of doctoring to be allowed to take it."

Miriam glanced up, and her hand stopped midway to the teacup. "What do—" But her hand didn't stop soon enough, because it struck something. Hard.

The awful sound of a dish clattering interrupted her words. She grabbed for the cup, as warm liquid seeped over her leg.

"Whoa, now." Alex caught the china teacup just before it hit the solid wood floor. What little liquid was left in the cup showered over his hand and white shirtsleeve.

"Ohhh." Gripping the tray handles, Miriam moved it to the other side of the bed to survey the damage. "Here, let me wipe your hand."

She took the teacup from him and placed it safely on the table. Then grabbed the cloth Alex had used to cover the tray, and rubbed it over his hand. "Your sleeve is soaked." She cradled his hand in the crook of her arm while she scrubbed at the fabric.

"Don't worry about it. Tea is one of the nicer things that's stained my shirtsleeve."

She looked up to gauge his level of annoyance, and caught a twinkle in his eye. And with her holding his arm, those eyes were close. Her breath caught. Flecks of red and yellow glittered in the brown of his gaze.

They both froze, awareness sparking between them. The moment stretched. At last, the Adam's apple bobbed in his throat, and he leaned back, sliding his arm from her grasp.

The movement snapped Miriam from her stupor. Dropping her focus to the bed, she scrubbed furiously at the wet spot in the gray wool blanket. "I'm so sorry." Her cheeks flamed hot enough to shoot off sparks.

"My fault. And I'm afraid you don't have any tea left." He smacked his forehead with his palm. "If I'd been thinking, I would've brought the whole pot from the café, not just a cupful. Can you ever forgive me?"

Forgive him? The man must think she was a clumsy schoolgirl, still growing into her limbs.

The wet patch on the blankets was as dry as she could

get it, so Miriam scanned the area to see if she'd missed anything.

The floor. A puddle sat next to the bed, right where the teacup would have landed and shattered in many pieces.

"Let me get that." Alex pulled the cloth from her hand and dropped to his knees.

Was he trying to make her feel worse? Not only had she made a mess, but now he had to clean it up? "I'm sorry, Doctor Donaghue. I don't know what came over me. I've never been this clumsy."

He looked up, a rakish grin pressing a dimple into one cheek. "On the contrary, m'lady. Your loveliness so overwhelmed me, I could do naught but drop to one knee."

Miriam stared at him, then realized her jaw had dropped open. She snapped it closed. Should she be offended? Mortified? Actually, what he'd said was a little funny. She bit back a smile.

Seconds later, he settled back in the chair, as if she'd not done anything strange or embarrassing. "So tell me, Miss Bryant, have you lived in the Montana Territory all your life?"

She picked up one of the sandwich quarters, and nibbled before answering. "Please call me Miriam. We moved to the mountain when I was five, from our farm in Kentucky." She scrunched her brow. "I don't remember Kentucky, though. My first memory is sitting behind Pa on his horse as he herded cattle." She glanced at him. "What about you? Did you grow up in Boston?"

"Yes, ma'am. Born above Dad's apothecary shop. All four of us were." He leaned forward, elbows on his knees. "I think my first memory might have been there, standing beside Mum's rocking chair, tickling Britt's feet when she was just a wee one. The lass was barely old enough to sit up, but it always made her smile."

The light that shone in his eyes sent a warmth through Miriam's chest. "Britt's your sister?"

A shadow seemed to cover his features. "Yes, Britt was three years younger than me, then Cathleen came three years after her. Cathy's still at home."

Something wasn't right here. The way his voice changed when speaking of his sisters. "Does Britt still live in Boston?"

He swallowed, the knob at his throat bobbing. "She died."

"Oh, Alex, I'm sorry." So that's why the light had left his eyes.

"Me, too." His voice rasped. "Anyhow, we all helped Dad in the shop. He taught us to love working with herbs and other naturals to help people. I suppose that's why Bryan and I both became doctors."

"And Cathleen, does she like healing, too?"

His mouth pinched in a thoughtful look. "She's more like Mum, likes doing things around the house. But I think Dad's hoping she'll take over the shop one day."

"Did you and your brother go to medical school in Boston?"

The corners of his eyes creased. "The McGill Faculty of Medicine in Montreal, Canada."

"Canada? But…" Miriam sifted through her memories of things Leah had said about the place. "Don't they speak French there?"

His eyes flashed and his mouth curved. "Oui, mademoiselle."

Miriam almost squealed. "You speak French?"

"Très peu. Very little." He leaned back in his chair. "I always thought it humorous that a couple of Irishman went to a French school, but..." He shrugged. "It worked out pretty well for Bryan, so who was I to argue?"

Alex was such a smooth talker, it was hard to tell sometimes whether he was joking or not. She raised her brows at him. "So you went there because your brother did? Hoping to pass grades because your teachers remembered him fondly?"

Alex winked, and the motion affected her all the way to the core of her stomach. "You've discovered my weaknesses, eh?"

His pause stretched so long, she wasn't sure if he'd give the real reason. "Seriously, it was an excellent school. Well respected, as were the physicians it produced. Prided itself on a four-year course, instead of the two years most medical schools require." He nodded. "I'll always be indebted for the knowledge I received there."

A long breath escaped him, as his gaze fell to the floor. "But I suppose it isn't always quite enough."

Mick Langley. Alex had seemed like his old self this afternoon, but the grief must be hiding under his façade.

Miriam reached forward to slip her hand over his. "You're still a talented doctor, Alex. You can only do your best, and let God take it from there."

His eyes rose to meet hers. "You've been talking to my brother, haven't you?"

"No, but I'm glad he sees the truth, too."

Alex turned his hand so hers slipped into his palm. It fit well there, and he covered it with his other hand. His brows knit, like he was putting great thought into his next words.

Before he could speak, a voice called from down the hall. "Alex." Doc Bryan's voice.

Alex gave her hand the slightest of squeezes before he

laid it on the cover beside her. "I suppose I should get back to work." Tucking an arm in front of him, he bowed low, slipping into his courtier's accent. "I hope you enjoy your lunch, m'lady. I'll be back for your tray directly."

Chapter Seven

*A*lex whistled a lively tune that evening as he carried the crate down the boardwalk from Aunt Pearl's Café. This was possibly his best idea yet. Although tea and sandwiches for Miriam's lunch had been a good one, too.

The aroma of rich gravy and meat wafted to his nose, setting his stomach to grumbling. "Settle down there," he mumbled, shifting the box to one hand so he could open the clinic door.

Bryan stood in the front room, reading a letter in his hand. He looked up when Alex entered. "Well, there's the benefactor now."

Alex ignored the tease in his tone. "Hungry? Thought you might appreciate Aunt Pearl's cooking better than mine."

Both of Bryan's brows rose. "Must be a holiday I've forgotten. First, Parker shows up with a table, saying you paid for it to be delivered. Now you're bringing in restaurant fare. Has Christmas come early?"

"Where'd you put the table?" Alex scanned the room. Not in here.

"In our quarters. Wasn't sure what you had in mind

for it."

Alex affected a casual air. "I thought it would be nice to put it in Miss Bryant's room. We haven't had a proper place to sit down and take a meal here. Now that she's feeling better, thought she might like company at meal times."

Bryan studied Alex, suspicion wafting off him like smoke from a fire. Finally, one corner of his mouth twitched. "All right." Then Bryan turned and strode down the hall.

Releasing a long breath, Alex watched him go. That hadn't gone as easily as he'd hoped. It was over, though. And it'd been worth it to make their patient more comfortable. She had to be lonely, staying in that room by herself all day. That was plain by the look in her eyes. Any little joy he could bring more than justified the effort.

He carried the crate of food toward Miriam's room, and met Bryan coming through the door that divided the clinic from their private sleeping chamber. Or rather, he met the table Bryan carried.

Stepping aside to let his brother enter Miriam's room first, Alex studied the table. It had a small square top, but plenty of room for three people to sit around it. The sturdy pine surface had been sanded smooth, and there was even a small decoration carved at the top of each of the four legs. Nothing fancy, but serviceable.

"What? Oh my." Miriam's voice drifted over the huge wood piece suspended in Bryan's grip.

Alex peeked around the edge, hoping for a glimpse of her reaction. She sat up in bed, loose blonde curls scattered around her face. Excitement glistened in her eyes. "What's it for?"

"We need a place to put this table. Mind if we keep it here?"

Her green eyes grew even wider. "Certainly."

Bryan set it down with a heave and a thud, then Alex set to work laying out dinner. "Do you mind company at meal times?" He forced himself to keep a casual demeanor, not looking her way.

"I'd be eternally grateful."

A smile tugged at his lips.

"That smells heavenly. Although after lying around here all day, I'm not sure I should be allowed to eat it."

"Come now." He sent her a wink. "Mending tendons and ligaments is a challenging business. As your physician, I prescribe rest and good food." He couldn't resist a grin. "Which is why I brought food from the café instead of forcing my own cooking on you. Do you like fried beef and gravy?"

"I like whatever's giving off that wonderful aroma."

Interesting to note she didn't argue the disparaging comment about his cooking. He couldn't blame her. After eating his gruel four mornings now, it was a wonder she hadn't lost her appetite.

A short while later, Alex and Bryan had pulled in chairs and sat around the table. They'd scooted it close enough to overhang the bed, so it was almost like Miriam sat at the table with them. He'd been pretty sure she might have trouble cutting the meat from her lower position on the bed, so Alex had asked the girl at the café to cut their steak portions before packing them. Did she notice the extra attention? Not that he wanted her to.

Conversation soon turned to their patients, as it usually did. Bryan relayed those he'd seen in the clinic that day.

"Mrs. Malmgren seemed rather put out that she had to see me instead of 'that charming Doc Alex.'" Bryan shot him a withering look. "I remember the day she was perfectly happy to be seen by an old boring chap like me."

"I suppose it's my charms she can't resist." Alex shot Miriam a grin, ducking to avoid the hand cloth Bryan aimed at his head.

"It certainly isn't your looks. It appears her vision is completely gone now."

Alex sobered. "Yes, I noticed that the last time she came in. She said her mother lost her sight at an even younger age. Sweet lady seems determined to make the best of it, though."

Bryan nodded. "I was surprised at how well she gets around. She's gotten good at using that cane you gave her. I'm still concerned about her staying by herself now that her husband's passed." He scraped the last bite from his plate, wiped his mouth with a cloth, and leaned back in the chair. "Best meal I've had in weeks." He smiled at Miriam. "If having you here means we get to eat decent food, Miss Bryant, you're welcome to stay on permanently."

The pink that stained her cheeks was a good color on her.

Bryan tossed the cloth on the table. "I need to catch up on case notes. You okay here, little brother?"

Alex tried to ignore a prick of annoyance at the old nickname. "Got it covered."

After he'd stacked the used dishes, Alex carried them to the next room over. Having their only cook stove in the primary exam room wasn't the best layout for their clinic. It kept the room warm for patients in the winter months, but tended to stir up dust and debris in an area that he tried to keep as sterile as possible. Maybe they should do something about that.

He made quick work of scrubbing the dishes in the

pot of water on the stove, allowing his mind to wander back through the evening. Miriam had seemed to enjoy the meal, especially the company. Too bad it ended so soon.

And then a new idea crept into his thoughts. Maybe there could be a legitimate reason to extend the evening. Did Bryan still have that box of dominos on the shelf in their room? But what was he thinking? It wasn't his job to entertain her. Only to make sure her injuries healed correctly. But wouldn't a pleasant evening help her mental health, which might help her body mend more quickly?

A few minutes later, he knocked on the wooden frame of Miriam's open doorway, domino box in hand. "Sorry to disturb, but I've a favor to ask."

She looked up, smoothing the covers over her legs. "Of course."

"I have an intense hankering for dominos, but I can't seem to pull Bryan away from his notes. Would you be interested?" He held up the carved wooden box.

Her eyes widened, reflecting the glow from the lantern. "That'd be wonderful. The perfect end to a perfect evening."

Warmth washed through his chest. His goal accomplished.

They divided the wooden pieces, and it soon became clear Miriam was having an unusually lucky evening.

After she won the third set, she gave him a narrow-eyed stare. "You're not even trying."

Alex raised his hands, palms out as if to ward off the accusation. "I am. To be honest I've never seen such a lucky streak." He raised his brows. "But I would never accuse a lady of cheating." He let the implied insinuation hang in the air for a moment, then winked to make sure she knew he jested.

Her eyes went wide, feigning extreme innocence. "Why, sir. Have you considered I may be just that talented?"

His mouth begged to grin, but he fought it as long as he could. Dominos weren't exactly a game of skill, but of anyone, she was clever enough for talent to be the reason behind her winning streak.

Alex won the next game, then of course Miriam triumphed in the one after that. As he flipped the dominos face down, her hand stole up to cover a yawn.

"Looks like I've overstayed my welcome." He began to line the dominos in the box. "Thanks for a delightful evening, though."

"Oh, no." She truly looked disappointed. "I don't know how I could be tired after lying in bed all day."

She was adorable, with that pert little nose and the way she got so frustrated with herself.

He gave her his most calming smile. "I shouldn't have stayed up so late myself. At the moment, sleep is what this doctor recommends for us all."

With the game put away and the table pushed into an empty corner, Alex stepped to the work counter where he'd stored a few medicines. "I'll prepare your arnica, then leave you in peace. Do you need anything for the pain?"

"No, my knee already hurts less."

Thata girl. No need to worry about Miriam becoming addicted to the laudanum. She was tough.

As he brought the small tincture of arnica to Miriam, his eyes drifted to the beautiful blonde curls sneaking from her braid. Did they feel as soft as they looked?

She handed the empty tumbler back to him with a smile. Her eyes shone a dark green. "Pleasant dreams, Alex."

He swallowed. Everything in him wanted to lean down and touch his lips to her forehead, or her soft hair, or better yet…

Forcing himself to turn away, he strode to the door. "Goodnight."

Miriam lay still, listening to the sound of male voices in the next room over. Doc Bryan's voice easy to pick out, so calm and methodical. It was probably reassuring to his patients, easing their fears with his unruffled manner. But how different he was from Alex, whose easy way of communicating disarmed and cheered everyone he spoke to. Even the burliest of miners. She nibbled her lip to hold back a smile.

The man whom Doc Bryan spoke with now had a working-class accent, but it was hard to tell what he said. Coughs interrupted every minute or two. They'd been in there for a while. Shouldn't they be done soon? She glanced out the window, where dusk had settled over the street. Each day now seemed a little shorter than the last.

Peering as far down the road as possible, she looked for Alex. Men passed both directions, mostly miners, along with a few businessmen. But not Alex. Since his brother came back to the clinic early today, Alex had left to run an errand. She allowed a sigh. All this waiting was driving her crazy.

Of course, it wasn't the Donaghue men's job to entertain her. Still, the last two evenings when they ate dinner together had become her favorite part of the day.

A few minutes later, the men's voices grew louder as Doc Bryan escorted the patient into the hallway toward the front door. The outside door opened, and Miriam strained to hear better. This laziness sure had made her nosy.

Another voice added to the mix, lilting with the smallest bit of an accent. Alex. Miriam's stomach flipped. This infatuation developing in her couldn't be good. But at least it helped pass the days, looking forward to Alex stopping by her room for a visit between patients. Soon, she'd be back up on the mountain where she could at least be useful.

And then in the spring…their trip East. Another sigh escaped. This one developing from happy thoughts. Traveling by boat and then train. Seeing all those fancy cities. Staying in hotels with servants to do her every bidding. Eating meals she never had to cook. It would be all her dreams come true. *Thank You, Lord.*

Footsteps sounded in the hall, jerking her out of the happy thoughts. Alex appeared in the doorway, his thick brown hair mussed from the wind. "I'll have dinner ready before you can sing 'Good-bye, Liza Jane.' Fried ham and eggs okay?"

"Perfect." A grin stretched her face. She should do a better job holding in her excitement.

Chapter Eight

$\mathcal{M}$iriam raised a bite of ham to her mouth and eyed the brothers. As usual, their dinner conversation revolved around patients. The two of them were so different, hearing and watching them interact never failed to captivate her.

"Two more men from The Original came in with trouble breathing." Bryan loaded a forkful of eggs into his mouth.

Alex's head jerked up. "Sound like fluid in the lungs?"

His brother nodded. "Mostly the same symptoms we've been seeing."

A fist slammed on the table, jerking Miriam's gaze to Alex. "Enough, Bryan. We have to find what's causing this."

Bryan gave him a long, calculating look. "Have you been down in the mines? Really seen the conditions? The men work a thousand feet underground. The tunnels start off cold, but when the men start working the temperature gets so hot they're dripping sweat. Then they come up to the surface at the end of the day, and the cold air freezes their clothes solid." Bryan's words gained momentum and volume as he went. "No wonder they're all sick. It's part of the job."

"That doesn't make it okay." Alex looked like he might leap from his chair and storm off to track down the mine owners.

"I know." Bryan emphasized every word. For the first time, she saw his calm façade start to slip.

"But what are we going to *do* about it? We have to help."

The breath left Bryan in a long stream. "I've talked to some of the mine barons, William Farlin and W.A. Clark. They didn't seem opposed to helping, as long as it doesn't affect their profits."

Alex braced his hands on the table, leaning forward. "What'd you tell them to do?"

Bryan shrugged. "Let the men come to the surface a couple times throughout the day, for one. That'd give them clean air to breathe every few hours." His forehead wrinkled. "It's not that easy, though. I talked to a couple of the miners, and they say riding the elevator is worse than staying locked underground. Said they don't wanna go up or down any more than necessary."

Miriam was doing her best to follow the conversation without interrupting, but Bryan's words might as well have been French for all the sense they made. "What's an elevator?"

He glanced at her. "The cage they use to bring the miners and the silver up and down. They cram a half dozen men in, then lower them down about a thousand feet into the main shaft. The whole time, the cage is rattlin' and shakin'. It's enough to make a man start praying." After scrubbing a hand over his face, his gaze settled far away. "I suppose I understand not wanting to ride the elevator too often. But there has to be another way."

Alex drummed his fingers on the table. "Do you think it's what they're breathing? What if we built some kind of mask that would purify the air before they inhale it?"

Bryan raised both brows at him. "And how do you suggest we do that?"

"I haven't the foggiest notion, but it'd be worth a try." Alex scooted forward, excitement rolling off him. "I'll write some men I knew in Montreal. They were creating special masks for patients to breathe ether during surgery. Maybe we could use the same idea to help here."

"I guess it's worth a try." Bryan still looked skeptical, but a tiny ray of hope also shown in his face.

Alex was almost beaming. He stood and stacked dishes. "I'll go start the letters now. Bryan, any chance you'd be interested in helping clean-up?"

Bryan pushed to his feet, offering Miriam a tight-lipped smile as he answered his brother. "Certainly."

The next day, Miriam only saw Alex for a quick greeting in the morning. Bryan stayed close to the clinic, busy with correspondence when he wasn't talking with patients. Another long, lonely day for her, cooped up in her little chamber.

It had been a week since the accident. A very long week, but her leg felt so much better. She still hadn't left the bed, except for awkward attempts to use the chamber pot. And that one time she'd hobbled to the door after Mick Langley died.

But if she didn't get up and move around soon, she may very well go out of her mind. She'd never gone so long without doing something useful. Maybe she could limp around the room and wipe the dusty work table and shelves. Or if she could get to the stove in the other room, it would be like heaven to cook again. Why had she ever hated that task? Alex's fare was edible, but after Leah's cooking for the last couple years, she craved something warm and savory. Not burnt and leathery.

A pretty pink color was just starting to stain the edge of the evening sky when Doc Bryan knocked on the door frame of Miriam's chamber. "I've been invited to dine with friends tonight, Miss Bryant, so I need to leave now. Alex should be back directly. Can I get you anything before I go?"

She forced her mouth into a smile. "No. Thanks, though." She picked up a well-worn copy of Joseph Maclise's *Surgical Anatomy* from her bedside table. "I'll do some light reading while things are quiet."

That brought a chuckle, which was an unfamiliar sound from Bryan. "All right then. Good evening."

But as soon as the front door closed, she tossed the book back on the table. If she saw another diagram of the human body, she might scream.

It wasn't long, though, before Alex arrived, coming to her relief as he'd done so many times these last few days. He stopped in her doorway, and she shared a pleasant smile. "Good evening."

But he didn't smile back. Instead, his mouth formed a grim line under the black smudges covering his face. His once-white shirt was streaked a muted gray, and his shoulders slumped in a way that made her breath catch.

"What's wrong?" She sat up in bed, wanting with everything in her to go to him. Wrap him in a hug and tell him it would be all right. What had him so defeated? And how could she help?

He leaned against the wooden door frame, as if he had to prop himself up. "I visited mines today." Even the simple statement seemed to wear him out.

She hesitated. He'd done that before hadn't he? Did he mean… "New mines?"

Alex shook his head. "No, the Alice and the Original. I went down in the shafts. I'd never done that." His tired eyes raised to meet hers, and the anguish there brought tears to sting the back of her throat. "It's awful, Miriam. The mines are so deep, it's like going to the center of the earth. When all the men start working, shafts must heat to over a hundred degrees, and there's dust everywhere. And this black coal-like powder gets on everything. No wonder the men are all sick." His whole body sank lower.

He was going to collapse right there if she didn't do something.

Miriam patted the edge of the bed beside her. "Come sit down."

He looked for a long moment at the spot where she pointed, as if debating whether he had the energy to reach it. Finally, he shuffled forward and sank onto the blanket. "I can't imagine working there day in and out. What a miserable life. And it's killing them."

Reaching for his hand, Miriam folded hers around it. "Is there anything we can do to change it?"

He raised his head, allowing her to stare into the bleakness in his dark eyes. "It would take a better man than me."

She squeezed his hand. "There can't be such a man in all the Montana Territory."

Their eyes locked for a long moment, and Miriam willed him to believe her words. He was such a good man. The depth with which he cared for others amazed her. How he took their struggles on himself, and did what he could to make things better.

Alex raised her hand to his lips and laid a gentle kiss on the curve of her fingers. "M'lady. If only it were true."

Miriam's chest constricted. What was it that made him think the worst of himself? If only he could see himself through her eyes.

The next morning, Alex poked his head in Miriam's room after he finished with his first patient. "You warm enough in here? The weather's dipping pretty chilly outside."

She'd been staring out the window, but turned those beautiful green eyes on him. "I'm watching the snow clouds roll in. I think it's going to be a bad one."

It was then he noticed the twin lines between her brows. Was she worried they wouldn't be safe here? They had enough food to last a few days, and surely they could walk to either the café or the dry goods store if the need arose.

She spoke again before he could set her mind at ease. "I wonder if Gideon and Leah are already on their way down."

The thought showered over him like a bucket of cold spring water. Her family might be out in this mess. And wouldn't the weather be worse up on the mountain?

Alex stepped into the room and perched on the edge of the chair beside her bed, hands clasped on his knees. "Do you think they would travel with bad weather coming?"

She nibbled her lower lip. "Gideon knows better, but

I'm afraid he might try to make it through the pass before it closes off."

Closed off? Did that mean... "How long does it take for the pass to open again after a snow?"

Her teeth worked harder on her lip, and the fingers on one hand clasped those of the other in a nervous action. "It depends. Sometimes a few weeks. If we have more storms, it may be all winter."

His fingers itched to reach out and untangle her worried hands. Not only was she concerned for her family's safety, she faced the very real possibility that she might be separated from them the entire winter.

Reaching out for her right hand, he pulled it onto his lap. "Your brother's one of the smartest mountain men I've ever met, Miriam." It didn't matter that he hadn't met that many yet. Bryan had told fabulous stories about the man's knowledge and skills. "Gideon won't take unnecessary chances. But I know if he can possibly come to you, he will."

She searched him with those intense eyes. Their outer edge a dark emerald, but the main circle around the iris glittering a lighter shade. Like the green garnet brooch Mum treasured that had been passed down through three generations of Irish mothers. Now, in this woman's eyes, he saw that same treasure. A spirit so priceless, it was made to be cherished.

Disappointment stabbed when she looked away, but that was probably for the best. Her eyes found the window again, and her mouth pinched. He needed to distract her.

"I was getting ready to make up more arnica tinctures and salves. Would you like to help?"

She swiveled to face him, hope filling her gaze. "Yes, please give me something to do."

He almost chuckled, but held it back. Moving to the

cabinet above the work counter, he pulled out a dozen small glass bottles, about the size of a small drinking glass. After placing those on the table beside Miriam, he brought over the tightly sealed jar of dried arnica leaves. "I picked and dried these when I first arrived in July. I'd never seen the arnica plants grow wild, just what we grew in the little gardens behind our shop."

As he showed her how many leaves to put in each tumbler, then the exact amount of gin to cover it with, Miriam's eyes studied his movements. "You have to be careful not to use too much of either ingredient. Arnica can be poisonous if ingested in high concentrations. And of course we don't want our patients intoxicated."

Her mouth formed a soft smile, and a twinkle flashed in her eyes.

After she crushed the remainder of the flower petals, he stirred them in a pot of oil and left it to simmer on the stove. "That will take several hours before it's ready, so I'll teach you how I add the new supplies into our inventory log."

As he showed her his method of adding and deducting medicines and materials in the ledger, she caught on within moments and quickly had the book updated. "I can handle all the recording if you'd like. That way you and Bryan don't have to worry about it."

He raised his brows. "You trying to put me out of a job?"

"You have more than enough to keep you busy. And I have nothing." She waved her hand over the bed, palm up. "You see any chores waiting? Please let me help."

Those eyes. He couldn't say no if he wanted to.

Chapter Nine

*F*inally a chance to help. Miriam sighed as she lay back against the cot. No matter that her efforts paled in significance compared to all the work the brothers did each day. Still, helping Alex infused her with a new sense of purpose.

Few patients came in that next morning, probably because of the impending storm. Only Mr. Crandall, and a miner's wife whom Alex said was expecting her first child in another month. After he brought Miriam a bowl of beef stew for lunch, Alex had said he had a quick errand to run. It was kind of him to ask whether she needed anything from the mercantile. She would have liked to give him a long list. Not the least of it being a few personal items—talcum powder, rose-scented soap, anything to supplement the sparse damp-cloth "baths" she'd been able to manage. But that would have to wait.

Now, flakes were starting to fall and both of the doctors traveled out in the weather. Surely Bryan would come home early today, wouldn't he?

And what of her own family? Would Gideon and Leah make it down the mountain before the storm hit? Did she want them to? No. As selfish as she was, she couldn't pray for them to be snowed in away from the ranch. What would the animals do without someone to break the ice for them daily? They'd die of thirst before they succumbed to starvation. It could mean total disaster for the ranch. Gideon wouldn't risk that. Relief washed over her shoulders. And maybe she could get used to the idea of being snowed in with her current company. A smile forced its way onto her mouth.

The squeaking hinges on the front door interrupted her thoughts. Her heart beat faster. At least one of the men was back.

"Alex?" Bryan's voice. So where was the younger Doctor Donaghue?

"He's gone to run an errand," she called.

Bryan's boots sounded in the hall, and his face appeared in the doorway. "He went out in this weather?" Twin lines creased his forehead. "The flakes are coming down thick. Does he know we could lose visibility if the wind picks up?"

A stab of fear pricked her chest. "He'll be back any minute."

Bryan looked uncertain. Would he go look for his brother? Surely Alex could handle himself in the snow here in town.

"How long ago did he leave?"

Miriam glanced outside. "I don't have a clock, but it's probably been an hour. I'm sure he'll walk in soon."

"We'll wait a few more minutes."

But Bryan had no patience. It must have been less than ten minutes before he donned his coat and gloves again. "I'm go—"

The squeak of the front door interrupted him. As Bryan stood in the hall outside Miriam's doorway, the thunder on his face gave away their visitor before Bryan spoke. "Have you lost your mind going out in this weather?"

"You were out, so it must not have been too bad." Alex's voice held a hint of challenge.

Bryan's face turned ruddy. "I've lived through a Montana winter. You haven't. With a strong wind, a heavy snow can turn deadly in minutes."

"I'm okay, Bryan." Alex came into sight as he spoke with a soothing calm. Nothing like the defiance from seconds before. He laid a hand on his brother's upper arm. "We're all safe. How about a mug of coffee? Feels like I should add wood to the stove, too."

Alex turned to flash a charming smile at Miriam. "Anything I can get you, Miss Bryant?"

"I'm fine, thank you." She murmured the words, but her gaze flicked back and forth between the brothers. Bryan stared at his brother with a stormy look in his eyes.

"All right then." Alex turned and retreated to the stove in the next room.

As Bryan watched him go, something about the slant of his jaw and the pinch of his lips no longer radiated anger. In this single unguarded moment, his mask split to reveal the fear that still clutched him.

Miriam's eyes flicked open, and she peered out the window beside her bed. A sheet of white greeted her, both on the ground and still falling from the sky. It seemed early still, but she studied the sky through the tiny holes in the curtain of flakes. Impossible to tell what time of day.

With a yawn, she stretched and pulled herself up to a sitting position. Scooting around, she finally found a comfortable situation that didn't press on the sore spot that had developed on her rump. If she never saw another bed, it would be too soon. Her eyes drifted to the Bible laying on the table. She should take time to read this morning.

The clank of iron sounded in the room next door. Were the men up already? Miriam quickly unfastened her braid, combed her fingers through the tangle of curls, and then rewove the plat. She was still tying the ribbon when a knock sounded on her door. "Come in."

Alex's face appeared as he eased open the door. The front of his hair was askew, and a shadow graced his jaw. Her stomach did a flip. The man was handsome at any time of day.

"Would you prefer coffee or willow tea this morning?" A hint of a smile touched the corners of his mouth.

"Coffee, please."

His brows rose. "Feeling better, are we?"

Miriam smoothed the covers with her hands, and turned her brightest smile on him. "Yes, I think I'm well enough to get up now."

One of his brows lowered, giving him a cockeyed look that properly conveyed his suspicion. "Out of bed, huh? We'll see about that."

Did that mean there was a chance? Miriam's heart soared and her hands clapped before she could stop them. "I'm ready. I know it."

He smiled, then disappeared from the doorway. Did that mean she'd be getting out of this infernal bed soon?

Alex reappeared with a mug of coffee, then left again without a word.

A half hour later, Bryan brought her a tray of dry biscuits and fried ham, along with a polite greeting. As she ate, the clinic stayed quiet. Eerily silent. Like the thick layers of snow outside had settled a dismal cloak over them all.

Had Gideon and Leah stayed on the ranch? She had to believe they wouldn't risk traveling with the storm coming.

The soft thump of boots sounded in the hall and Bryan appeared in the doorway. "Miss Bryant, this is probably a good time to examine your knee again. Need to make sure it's healing right. Is that acceptable?"

"Um...yes. Certainly." She swallowed. Now that she wasn't in so much pain—and knew the doctors a little better—it seemed strange to bare her knee in front of them.

"All right, then. Let me gather a few supplies."

Maybe it would just be Doc Bryan doing the examination this time. Heat crawled up her neck anyway.

A few minutes later, Doc Bryan stepped into the room carrying a tray of supplies and bandages. Followed by...Alex. So much for just one doctor. He sent her a smile before turning to the work counter that lined the wall.

"Let's have a look. Shall we?" Bryan stood over her as Miriam pulled the cover off her wrapped knee. His forehead wrinkled as he unwrapped the leather strips holding the stiff rawhide splint over her joint. When the bandages were removed, he peered at the long gash in her pale skin.

Miriam sucked in her breath. It was the first time she'd actually seen the wound. The slash spanned longer than her fingers. And red. Too red? She glanced up at the men's faces. Alex had stepped over to join his brother in the examination. Their brows furrowed, but they didn't look too grave. Did they?

The suspense was enough to drive her mad. "So what do you think?"

Alex touched the skin around the incision. Then he fingered the thread and quills he'd used to stitch the wound together. His focus on the area remained intense. He didn't even look to be breathing.

His finger brushed a sore spot, and Miriam jerked before she could stop herself. His head popped up and his brows drew low. "Sorry."

"It's all right. I won't move again."

He scanned the wound. "I think we're done here. In another week we'll take the stitches out and I'll have you start exercises. But for now try to keep it still. The incision looks good. No infection or heat that I can tell."

Miriam released a long breath, and with it the tension that had been building for days.

His eyes creased at the corners as he started wrapping a clean bandage around the wound. "Glad that's over?"

Her heart felt ten pounds lighter, and she allowed a smile to bloom on her face. "Glad it's healing."

"All right then. I've some work to do next door." Bryan waved the direction of his and Alex's private quarters as he backed out of the room.

With the splint wrapped firmly, Alex gathered the used bandage and supplies. He surveyed the bed and the work counter, as if looking for tools he missed. "I'll be back shortly." And he strode out of the room.

The silence stretched as time crawled by. Hadn't Alex said he'd come back soon? At long last, the door separating their chamber from the clinic creaked, and boots thumped on the wooden floor. Alex entered with a small paper bundle under his arm. "Sorry for the delay. Bryan was working on something quite interesting." A twinkle flashed in his eyes. "I suspect you'll think so, too. Anyhow, I found this and thought you might think it worth your time." He held the package out to her.

Even before her hand closed on it, Miriam had no doubt what it contained. "A book?" She fingered the rough brown paper, then clutched it to her chest. "Thank you, Alex. Oh, thank you."

A chuckle reverberated in his chest. "Open it."

Her hands fumbled with the wrapping, then smoothed over the marbled vellum cover of the book. *Emma* was printed in large gold letters on the leather spine, and underneath it *Jane Austen*. She raised her eyes to Alex's face. "Where did you get it?"

He slipped his hands in his pockets and shrugged, but the excitement shining in his eyes gave him away. "Oh, just found it somewhere."

She raised both brows. "Found it? In an old trunk left over from medical school?"

He ducked, red creeping into his cheeks. "Something like that."

Miriam's gaze fell back to the book and roamed over it. "Leah and I read some of Miss Austen's other works, and Leah told me about this one. But I've never had the chance to read it." Her eyes crept back up to his, and moisture burned her throat. "Thank you, Alex. A thousand times, thank you."

"You're welcome." He met her gaze and his own eyes glistened. Then he cleared his throat. "I, uh, need to catch up on some case notes. Would you like me to work in here?" He glanced around the little room. "Keep you company?"

His kindness knew no end. "I'd love that."

While Alex went to get his work, Miriam opened the book and immersed herself in the world of Miss Emma

Woodhouse and the easy life of the wealthy English upper class. She almost didn't realize when Alex came back in and settled at the table with his ledger, quill, and inkpot.

The relationship between Emma and Miss Taylor, her former governess and dearest friend, reminded her how close she and Leah had become. What she wouldn't give to have known Leah during her younger days. "And Highbury sounds wonderful."

"What's that?"

Miriam's head jerked up at the words. "What?"

His brow wrinkled in confusion. "You said something about a high surrey being wonderful."

Heat rushed into Miriam's face. "I, um… I said Highbury sounds like a wonderful place to live." She lifted the novel. "Where Miss Woodhouse grew up." Her eyes focused on the page. "A 'large and populous village, almost amounting to a town.' And within a half day's travel from London, too. Can you imagine?"

Alex's eyes squinted, as if he looked far away. "I've heard of Highbury, I think. Dad had a cousin who married an Englishman. They still live there, as far as I know." He glanced around the small, rustic room. "Although I suppose it's been a few years since I've heard news of her."

A cousin in England? So near to London, with its high fashion and gay parties? A sigh escaped her. "I've always wanted to visit London. Does your cousin attend balls and festivities there?"

He shrugged. "Haven't the faintest. Her husband's the miller in Highbury, so I doubt they're too high up the social scale." His mouth tipped, revealing a dimple. "Sorry to disappoint."

That familiar heat crept to her neck, so she dipped her head back to the book. "No disappointment. I'll let you get back to your work."

As Miriam read the next few sentences, the author quickly drew her back into the story. Such quick prose, you could never guess what funny statement would come next. And Mr. Knightley—even with only a quick introduction, Miriam was already falling in love. His charming wit made her want to giggle at some of his all-too-honest remarks.

"What's so funny?"

Miriam glanced up at Alex. "Funny?"

His face held a mixture of humor and frustration. With his brows raised, one side of his mouth pinched, and the other pushing a dimple into his cheek. The look pulled a grin from Miriam.

"You were laughing. Is the book that good?"

"Honestly, it is. I've always wanted to be a grand English lady, like Miss Woodhouse in the story." She quirked a brow at him. "And you can be Mr. Knightley, if you like."

Alex frowned. "I'd have to read the book to see if I like." He tipped his head, examining her. "You may not be English, but I think you have the lady part down. If you don't mind me saying so."

Did he really just call her a lady? Her cheeks must be blood red by now. But if he saw her at work on the ranch, he certainly wouldn't repeat his comment. Killing chickens for dinner. Hand feeding the baby calves when they couldn't nurse from their mothers. Tanning deer hides for leather. Her gaze rose to meet his. "Do you have any idea how I was injured, Alex?"

"You were mauled by a mountain lion."

She took a deep breath and released it. "Yes. I was hunting and had taken down a good-sized buck. I'd slit the hide to bleed it, and should have done a better job watching around me. The cat attacked to get me out of the way so he could claim the better prize."

She dipped her head. What would he think now? It was a far cry between an upper class English lady and a half-wild mountain woman who bled deer and fought off mountain lions. Of course, that wasn't what she did most of the time. Gideon usually did the hunting. She'd only taken the shot at the deer because she'd come across it on her way back from gathering willow bark. Still. Most of her chores were just as inglorious.

Footsteps sounded on the floor boards. Was he leaving? But his rough leather boots appeared in her vision, and Miriam raised her head to face him.

Alex perched on the edge of the seat beside the bed. He leaned forward, elbows resting on his knees. "Miriam, my opinion of a lady is not someone who sits around a drawing room and gossips all day. I believe a lady is someone who works hard for the good of others. Is kind and caring and fun to be around. Just like the woman from Proverbs thirty-one. Have you read it?"

She held his gaze, riveted there by the amber and green flecks in those deep brown eyes. Slowly, she nodded. It had been a while, though. She'd definitely read it again now.

His hand slipped forward to take hers, his thumb stroking the back of her fingers in a way that sent shivers down her arms. "Miriam, in my mind, you're the exact picture of that lady."

Moisture burned the back of her eyes. How did he see her so completely? It was like he understood both the woman she was, and who she wanted to be. And he didn't find either person lacking. But could she become the lady she wanted to be?

She swallowed, trying to find words to answer. Nothing came, especially not with those wide eyes still searching hers.

Chapter Ten

A voice cleared in the distance, and Alex stiffened. He released Miriam's hand, then slowly turned to face his brother in the doorway.

Miriam slipped behind Alex's profile so the heat had time to leave her face. What must Bryan think about finding them so close together? For that matter, what should she think? Was it improper? Maybe. And besides, she was probably just a diversion for Alex. When she left the clinic and went back up the mountain, would he have more than a passing thought of her?

"Sorry to interrupt, but I have them ready. The, uh..." Bryan cleared his throat. "The tools for Miss Bryant."

Alex jumped to his feet, scooting the chair aside. "Perfect."

From behind the door jam, Bryan drew two long wooden poles with short pieces of wood attached crossways at the top. Recognition flashed through Miriam. They were almost the same as Gideon had made for Leah when her leg was broken.

"Walking sticks." A smile spread across her face, and she looked up at Alex. "Does that mean I can get out of bed?"

His brows lowered. "Only for a few minutes at a time. Don't put any weight on your left leg. And if it pains you, go right back to the cot. Agreed?"

"Of course." She would've agreed to cut her hair short if that would get her out of this bed.

Bryan lowered her bad leg to the floor, helping to keep the knee straight. She tried to shake out her skirts, but they were hopelessly wrinkled. As her bare feet hit the wood planks, she almost squealed and pulled them back up. *Cold.*

Alex frowned. "We'll need to get you new..." Blotches of red stained his cheeks. "I mean, something to cover your...er, to keep you warm." Even his embarrassment was charming, as he stumbled around trying not to mention her unmentionable clothing and body parts.

"Let me have them." She reached for the walking sticks. With one under each arm—and a doctor by each side—she wobbled to her feet. Make that foot. A surge of pain shot through her knee, and her whole body ached like she hadn't used it in a month. But she was standing. She didn't try to stop the grin from showing on her face.

Miriam shuffled the left pole forward and shifted her weight to move with it. This was harder than it looked that time Leah used them.

"Easy there. Steady." Alex crooned like a nervous mare with her first foal, his hand cupping her right elbow.

She ignored him, easing the other crutch forward with her right leg. That was it. Getting her balance and not putting weight on her bad leg would be the hardest part, but each step grew easier.

She'd almost made it to the door when Alex spoke again. "I think that's far enough. You don't want to overdo it this first time."

But she kept moving forward, pulling out of Alex's grip on her elbow. "Just let me go to the next room and I'll sit."

"Miriam."

She ignored him, progressing faster now. If she moved both walking sticks ahead at the same time, then swung her body forward, she could get a good rhythm. Out in the hall, then into the examination room next door. She paused to take in her surroundings like a starved baby. How wonderful to be out of that little chamber.

Swinging forward again, she aimed toward a chair on the far wall. "See, I'll just sit here for a while."

Neither man had left her side, except when the doorway forced them to walk single file. When she reached the chair, Alex caught her elbow in a grip strong enough to slow her down. "Let us help you turn and sit." His voice held stern tension she'd never heard from him.

Had she pushed too far? Made him angry? A niggle of guilt tugged in her chest. "All right." They each took an arm and swiveled her as she pivoted on her good foot, then eased into the chair.

Sinking against the straight wood back, her body sagged. Just that little bit of activity had her working to catch her breath.

But now was the time for recovery of a different kind. She turned her most charming smile on the men who stared down at her like palace guards. Alex had both hands perched on his hips, brows knit so close they almost looked like a continuous line.

"That was dangerous, Miriam." His chest heaved with the words. "You could have fallen or reinjured the tendons." He threw up both hands. "Who's to say you didn't?"

Miriam couldn't hold his gaze. She'd really scared him. Not what she'd meant to do. Of course, she hadn't been thinking about anything other than the joy of getting out of that room. "I'm fine, Alex. I promise."

"Let's get you back to bed."

Her head jerked up. "No."

His face slipped again into the scowl.

"I mean, may I just sit here for a few minutes? You can go about your business, and I'll enjoy the new scenery. If I grow tired, I promise I'll call you for help getting back to bed."

Alex's gaze flicked from her face to his brother's, his mouth twisting with the question.

Bryan only raised his brows at his brother, as if to say, *It's your decision.*

Alex finally turned back to her. "All right. Five minutes. And *don't* go back to the other room without one of us. Understood?"

"Thank you." If he'd been closer, she would have pulled him down into a hug.

He held her gaze a moment longer, and his mouth twitched as if he could read her thoughts.

A movement in the corner of her eye ended the moment. Miriam turned as Bryan stepped to the stove. "I'll get the coffee heating." When he'd refilled the firebox and moved the kettle forward, Bryan turned to clap Alex on the shoulder. "Can I get your help for a minute, little brother?"

"Sure." Alex gave her one more warning look before turning to follow.

Miriam feasted her eyes on her surroundings. The work counter and long row of cabinets on the side wall, where most of the medicines and supplies stayed. The high examination table in the center. She had a faint memory of it being extremely hard, almost like lying on a piece of wood. Even the window behind her offered a different view of the large icy flakes still gliding from the clouds.

A hazy moisture crept over the window, both where she breathed on the glass, and around the edges. Must be the warmth from the fire. Miriam pulled at the collar of her shirtwaist. It *was* toasty in here. The wood Bryan loaded in the stove was doing its job.

Her eyes fell on the open heater vent, wide enough that she could see the orange flames dancing inside. The stove was too far away for her to reach from the chair, but if she stood, one step would bring her close enough to shut the vent. Positioning the walking sticks under her arms, Miriam pulled herself up. She stopped to steady her balance, then rocked forward on the poles, landing an easy distance from the stove. Keeping the pole under her left arm for support, she leaned the other stick against the wall. With a few flicks of her wrist, she had the vents closed, drowning out the crackling of the fire along with the heat.

A gurgling sound drifted from the top of the stove. *The coffee.* With the towel hanging from the stove handle, she moved the kettle to a cooler part of the iron surface. The aroma was tantalizing. How many hours had it been since she'd finished her cup that morning? Taking a tin mug that hung from the stove's upper shelf, Miriam set it on the side counter then reached for the kettle. Its handle was hot to the touch, so she wrapped the towel around it again.

The pot was heavier than she expected, and Miriam's wrist strained under the weight. Her body tilted forward to compensate, and she brought her left hand down to brace herself against the warming counter. The supporting crutch under her left arm slipped.

And then everything seemed to happen in slow

motion, yet she was powerless to stop it. The kettle clattered against the stove top, her hand still clutching the handle. Her midsection hit the edge of the stove, and she hovered over the surface.

A searing pain exploded over her left arm. Like fire burning her skin. She tried to cry out. To scream. To claw the burning pain away.

Strong hands gripped her shoulders, pulling her back. Her vision blurred and voices buzzed around her, but nothing made sense. She had to get away from the agony blazing across her arm.

And then her arm was submerged in a blessed coolness. Icy bliss. She blinked, forcing her eyes to focus through the pain. The first thing she saw…Alex.

"Shhh, love." He stroked the hair from her face. His wide brown eyes glistened as he met her gaze.

Something tugged at her arm, reigniting the burning sensation. She looked over. Bryan bent over her arm, a long shiny knife in his hand. Miriam gasped and jerked back.

"Steady now. He's cutting your sleeve so we can get to the burn." Alex's voice crooned in her ear as he moved to her side, wrapping his arm behind her. Did his hands shake? Or was that the chatter of her teeth?

She bit into her lower lip, doing her best to not react to the pain of the fabric pulling her skin. She shrank into Alex's chest, and he held her securely there. The cloth of his shirt was damp against her cheek, and only then did she realize tears streamed down her face.

As Bryan's knife cut through the last of the fabric, the cloth fell apart. Miriam blinked, but the mottled red skin didn't change. Was that her arm? He cupped her elbow and lowered her hand into a basin of snow, scooping more slush over her forearm.

Heavenly relief flooded her, and she inhaled a deep breath. The biting cold of the ice almost masked the burning in her arm. As her muscles relaxed, she sank deeper into Alex's arms.

Alex cradled Miriam against his chest, willing his heart to stop racing. He closed his eyes, but the memory rushed back. Hearing her scream. Finding her crumbled on the floor, holding her arm and whimpering. He forced his eyes open. Inhaling a deep breath, he rocked the woman in his embrace. She still smelled like coffee, but her hair was soft against his cheek.

Beside him, Bryan rose to his feet. "I'll get more snow."

"Laudanum first?" Alex spoke softly so he didn't disturb Miriam, who had finally calmed in his arms.

Bryan paused mid step. "Good thinking."

As Bryan stooped to give Miriam a hefty dose of the medicine, Alex caught a glimpse of her face. Anguish pooled in her eyes. It pressed his chest so tight, breathing became painful.

Burying his mouth in the blonde curls near her ear, he whispered, "I'm sorry, love. If I could take this pain for you, I would."

While Bryan left to gather more snow, Alex ran his eyes over the situation before him. They needed to get Miriam back in bed. Both legs lay straight in front of her, as far as he could tell with her skirts covering them. Maybe God had been merciful and kept her from reinjuring her knee in the fall.

The burn on her arm was a bad one. Before Bryan covered it with ice again, he'd glimpsed blisters rising on the surface. If they didn't get her arm medicated and wrapped with bandages soon, the blisters might burst. And the infection that would surely ensue could easily take either her arm or her life. Alex tightened his hold. A burn like this was serious.

When his brother reappeared, Alex carefully pulled away from Miriam, while keeping an arm at her back to keep her upright. "Miriam, I'm going to carry you back to your room. Bryan will walk beside to hold the ice for your arm. All right?"

She nodded once, her teeth starting to chatter. Was she cold? Going into traumatic shock?

He touched two fingers to her neck. The blood flow there pulsed fast but not very strong. Getting her warm was priority now.

With careful balance, he cradled Miriam and rose to his feet. Bryan gripped the basin of ice on her other side, and helped position her injured leg so Alex's arm supported it properly.

Within moments, he laid her on the bed and pulled both the quilt and the gray wool blanket up around her chin. He eased the burned arm and basin to a safe place on top of the blankets. "We need more quilts."

Moments later, Bryan thrust two blankets in his hands. They worked together to apply a strong healing ointment to the burn and wrap it in clean cloth strips. The scalding liquid appeared to have burned through two layers of skin. By the time Alex tied the bandage ends together, Miriam had stopped shivering and her eyelids drifted shut.

"I'll clean up the other room," Bryan murmured as he slipped away.

"Feeling better?" Alex spoke softly as he stroked a lock of curls from Miriam's face.

"Mmm." Her voice was barely a whisper, and her eyes remained closed.

"Sleep now. I'll be here when you wake."

She didn't answer, but her breathing drifted into a steady rhythm. Before he could stop himself, he leaned down and pressed a kiss to her forehead.

Miriam murmured something, as if from a dream. Was that his name? Or wishful thinking?

"Alex." Louder this time, so there was no doubt.

"Yes?" But again, no answer. Her lashes fluttered, as if her mind was busy under those delicate lids. Was she dreaming about him? Warmth flooded his chest.

Chapter Eleven

*M*iriam struggled to force her eyes open. This fogginess in her mind was worse than wading through waist-high snow. As her eyelids cracked, harsh white light set her head to aching again.

"Aww…" She moaned, raising her hand to shield her face from the brightness streaming through the window. A throbbing ache enveloped her arm, leaving her gasping through the pain.

The burn. It all came back in a torrent of anguish. Memories of pain everywhere—in her arm and her knee. So strong she could only thrash and moan. Cool cloths on her face, gentle fingers stroking her hair. Alex, soothing in that rich, magical voice of his. They helped, but nothing took away the pain.

But waking up now, the throbbing in her arm wasn't quite as strong. Had it been a full night then, and now they were into the next day? A wagon rattled by outside, and she craned her neck to see through the window. Snow still packed several inches higher than the window sill, but muddy slush covered the road, and men and horses passed in steady succession. The red door of the legal office across the street winked through the traffic.

Murmuring voices drifted from the other room. Alex's deep tenor was unmistakable. A woman's voice sounded, too. Older maybe. Alex chuckled, and even muffled by the wall, the sound washed through her in warm ripples.

Miriam lay there, listening for several moments, as the voices rose and faded. When the hinge on her door creaked, she startled. "Yes?" Her voice was still groggy from sleep, and from the cotton that seemed to cling inside her mouth.

Alex's head appeared in the doorway. "You're awake?" At first his eyes widened, then his brow lowered into a worried furrow as he strode across the room to her bed. "Would ye be feeling better, now?" His hand touched her forehead.

"Much better." She tried to offer a smile, but it must have been a weak one.

He stepped back, eyes roaming over her face. "Your fever is gone. Let me help our Mrs. Malmgren out, then I'll be back."

While she waited, Miriam's eyes drifted shut again. How much could one sleep in a day? Surely she'd napped enough this past week to last for several months.

She jerked awake to find Alex entering her room, a tray in his hands with steam wafting from a bowl.

"Hungry yet?"

With the savory aroma of soup filling the air, the cramping in her stomach gave her a decisive answer to that question. "I am."

As he placed the tray on the bedside table, he gave her one of those crooked grins. "I imagine so. You haven't eaten in two days."

Her eyes jerked to the window, where the sun still shone brightly. Two days? Finding Alex's gaze again, she was almost afraid to ask the question. "Is something wrong with me?"

His brows rose. "You mean besides a torn patellar tendon and a second degree burn covering your wrist?"

"Would that make me sleep so much?"

Alex sank into the chair beside the bed. The smile left his face, and for a few moments she could see through his perky façade. He'd been worried. And now he was exhausted. "You kept a high fever after the burn. You weren't actually unconscious, but very feverish. We gave you plenty of laudanum for the pain, so that also contributed to your sleeping so much." He ran a hand through his unruly hair. "It's good to see you awake now. And without the fever."

As if coming awake, he lurched to his feet and reached for the tray. "Now, you need nourishment. Would you like me to feed you?"

Heat warmed her neck. Surely she was capable of doing that herself. "I can."

After positioning the tray across her lap, Alex settled back on the edge of the chair. Less than an arm's reach away. Was he worried she'd make a mess of this like she had the coffee?

The beef stew tasted better than some of the other meals Alex had served. Her eyes raised to meet his, as he watched her. "Did you make this?"

His brows gathered. "Is it that bad?"

"No, actually. It's quite tasty."

Red stole up his neck. "I'm learning."

Poor guy. She hadn't meant to embarrass him. "Is this

your mum's Irish stew you told me about?"

His face flushed a deeper crimson. "Not exactly. More like Aunt Pearl's recipe she was kind enough to share."

Miriam couldn't hold back a chuckle. As her upper body shook from the laugh, the tray tilted to the side, and she grabbed it. Best focus on eating before she triggered another disaster.

Eating was a little awkward with her left hand bandaged, but not too bad. Raising the bound arm, she asked, "How long will this need to stay wrapped?"

"At least until the blisters are gone. Several days, probably. We'll check it later today and see how it's healing."

When she lowered her arm to the bed, the loose, tattered edge of her sleeve flopped. "Looks like I'll need a new shirtwaist." She sighed. And a bath. Maybe she could ask for a bowl of water and a rag. Every part of her felt sticky and dirty.

Drawing forth her nerve, along with a deep breath, she didn't meet his gaze. "Would it be too much trouble to ask for a basin of water and a towel?"

"No trouble." He jumped to his feet and strode out of the room.

She hadn't meant right this minute. Still, the sooner the better. After scarfing down the remaining stew, she moved the tray to the side table before he returned.

Boot thumps sounded his coming, and Miriam ran a hand over her hair to push wayward curls behind her ear.

A wide smile stretched across Alex's face as he entered, giving him a school-boy look. He set down the basin and pulled a brown paper package from under his arm. Like a lad bringing flowers to his mother, he presented the bundle. "I thought you might be in need of this."

Miriam could feel her eyes widen. A package? A gift?

But why?

He couldn't quite meet her eyes, and red ears peeked out from under his dark brown locks as he turned to the table. "I'll take this tray and give you some privacy." Then his gaze flicked back to hers, his face growing serious. "Call if you've a need. I'll be close by. *Don't*...do anything dangerous."

"Yes, doctor."

His mouth tugged at her sassy reply, but he didn't answer as he left the room.

Miriam's fingers fumbled with the paper until she found the slit. The flexibility of the bundle meant it had to be fabric, right? As the wrapping fell away, she gasped. A cream-colored shirtwaist lay folded on top, with beautiful crocheted lace gathered in rows across the front and back. It was one of the most gorgeous creations she'd ever seen.

When she held the blouse up for a better look, a dark mossy green material peeked out from underneath. More? Lifting the wool material out, it unfolded into a long ready-made skirt. Pleats across the front gave the waist a tapered look while allowing the hem to hang full.

Together, the two formed a lovely outfit. And just her size from the look of them. Had Alex picked them out? She bit her lip. Hopefully, he'd put them on the Bryant Ranch's tab at the store, not paid out of his pocket. Surely.

Raising the blouse again, she examined every detail. The lace was exquisite. She hugged it to her chest. *Oh, thank you, Lord.*

It was much harder than she'd imagined to wash and dress while sitting in bed, and with her left hand wrapped in a bandage. But Miriam took her time, indulging in the sweet bliss of being clean again. And the clothes—even the slight scratch of the wool where it brushed her leg was a welcome nuisance. She took the time to unbraid her hair and wrap it in a knot at the top of her head. With only the ribbon to secure it, her wild tresses probably wouldn't stay in place for long. But at least she could feel stylish for a little while.

About a half hour passed before a knock sounded again on her door.

"Come in." Miriam straightened the blankets across her skirt.

Alex's face appeared as he cracked the doorway. "Just popping in to see if you need anything." His eyes widened and he stepped into the room. "You're...it's... beautiful. I mean..."

Miriam couldn't quite meet his gaze, so she glanced down at the dainty lace. "It's lovely, Alex." Forcing herself to look at him, she let her smile show. "I can't tell you how wonderful it is to have clean clothes. New clothes, I mean." She was making a mess of this. "Thank you."

At first he didn't answer, but the Adam's apple in his throat bobbed. "You're welcome." What was going on behind those glistening brown eyes? Did he regret the purchase? Was he disappointed in the way she looked in the clothes? Why did she even care what he thought?

At last he spoke, his voice thick. "I've never seen anything so lovely." He turned and strode from the room.

Chapter Twelve

Alex watched Miriam from the doorway of the front waiting room as she poured coffee into cups for the two men waiting. She'd healed quickly over the last few days, especially after they removed the stitches and she started strengthening exercises. Now, she moved around with the crutches like she'd used them all her life. It still unnerved him to see her so active, especially with her knee injury only two weeks old. But trying to keep her still was like taming the wildcat that attacked her. Not worth attempting for long.

"Here's coffee poured for you, sirs. I'm sorry I can't carry the cups."

"Not a problem, missy." The burlier of the two men rose from his simple wooden waiting chair and clomped toward the sideboard. "I can do the totin' fer ya."

As the man took both tin cups in his massive hands, he leaned close to Miriam and mumbled something under his breath. Alex stiffened. Anything that couldn't be said out loud was likely not proper to speak in a young lady's ear.

The burly man chuckled as he carried a mug to the frail man hunched in another seat. Miriam's face flushed pink, and Alex's fists clenched before he could stop them. This man was a patient. He had to remember that. But if the lout laid a finger on Miriam for any reason…

"Whoever's next can follow me." He never took his eyes from the burly miner, as the man turned and ambled toward him.

"Need an elixir, doc."

Alex ignored him until they were both in the examination room and he'd closed the door. "What's the trouble?" His words came out sharper than they should have. *Warmth, sympathy and understanding, Donaghue. Remember your Hippocratic Oath.* Inhaling a deep breath, he tried to force his face into a pleasant expression. "And what's your name, sir?"

The miner already had one boot on the edge of the exam table, and was rolling up his pant leg. "Baxter. My leg's botherin' me somethin' fierce."

And it was soon clear why. A deep red mark gouged the back of the fellow's calf at least the width of a man's hand. As Alex peered closer, it seemed to be a simple cut that had become quite infected. "How did this happen?"

A heavy cough drifted through the wall from the waiting room, pulling Alex's attention as he waited for Baxter to reply.

The man only shrugged. "Couldn't say."

"How long's it been red like this?"

Another lift of the shoulders. "'Bout a week."

Alex turned to the cabinets over the work table and gathered ingredients to make a poultice. He'd need a silver nitrate elixir for the infection, too.

While he worked, the cough from the miner in the next room continued to sound every minute or two, spurring Alex to move faster. He could still picture the man's thin shoulders. Did he have the same lung illness they'd been seeing?

In less than five minutes, he'd cared for Baxter's wound and given him instructions for the next few days. A niggle of remorse pricked his chest as he escorted the man back to the waiting room. He didn't usually rush in his care of a patient. He'd certainly done everything necessary with Baxter's wound, but his bedside manner may have been hurried.

Still, from the few glimpses he'd had of the frail miner, the man's condition could be a case of life and death. And he would *not* lose another patient.

Miriam released her pent-up air when Alex appeared in the hallway with the giant of a man. The frequent labored coughs of the poor miner in the chair tightened her nerves more than the cinch on a saddled horse. If only there was something she could do to help this poor man. Alex would have something, though.

Alex strode straight toward him, bent down so he was eye-level with the slumped figure, and extended his hand. "I'm Doc Alex. Let's get you back to the examination room and see what we can do."

The man was weak enough that he allowed Alex to wrap a supporting arm around him as they hobbled down the hall.

Miriam's gaze followed until both men disappeared around the corner. Alex was so good with his patients. The care and passion with which he doctored each left no doubt he'd found his calling. God had created this man to be a physician.

A shuffling sound brought Miriam's attention around. The big burly miner. What was he still doing here?

"Can I help you, sir?" Had he left and come back?

But as he approached, something about the squint in his eyes and the curve of his mouth under the trim beard made the little hairs on Miriam's neck rise.

He didn't answer, but she found herself moving a step backward with her crutches. The solid mass of the sideboard stopped her retreat.

"Do you need the doctor again?"

He released a soft chuckle. "No, ma'am. But I have a powerful need for a purty thing like you."

"I, um, I'm afraid I can't help you." Her voice came out a high squeak. Could he smell her fear the same way horses did? She had to get a handle on her emotions. Clearing her throat, she spoke more forcefully. "If you don't need the doctor, you should leave, sir."

He stood close now, towering no more than two feet away. His lower lip protruded in a fake pout. "What fun would that be?" And then a twinkle lit his black eyes. "Unless yer comin' with me."

"No." She pushed back against the solid wood behind her. "Please go."

"Come now, missy. We'll just have a little fun." He leaned close enough for his nauseating breath to cloud her face.

Miriam fought to hold in a cough. When his rough hand touched her jaw, her whole body went rigid.

"I'll make it pleasant for you." That snarly grin sent goose bumps down her back. "Very pleasant. Even with yer bum leg." His eyes lowered as if motioning to her crutches. But they landed on her chest and held several seconds.

Past the high neckline of her blouse, heat surged into Miriam's face. "Leave, sir. Or I'll call the doctor." With her left hand tightly gripping one crutch, she pushed hard on his chest with her right. Hopefully that would knock him off balance and she could scoot under his arm. But he didn't even sway. What a giant of a man. *Lord, help!*

Miriam opened her mouth to scream, but his coarse hand clamped tight over her lips. The foul odor of unwashed body convulsed her stomach.

His other hand clamped around her waist, jerking the air from her lungs. Both walking sticks clattered on the floor, and she fought hard to free herself from his grasp. She needed her good leg to support her and her burned wrist was almost worthless, so she pounded against his chest with her single strong fist.

The blighter had her body pressed tight to his, and started dragging her toward the door. Curses mixed with his disgusting breath.

Terror welled up in Miriam's chest like a wild animal, clawing for escape. She pummeled his face and chest for all she was worth, but this man was more than twice her weight. What could she do?

Alex pressed the chest piece of his stethoscope against Frank's lungs again. Yes, the inhalation was easier now that he'd given the man elecampane. But he'd need to keep him here a few days to stabilize his temperature and breathing.

Pulling back, he met the man's weak gaze. "Frank, we're going to do our best to get you better. I need you to spend a few nights here at the clinic, though. All right?"

The weary pale blue eyes of the old miner dropped to the floor as he nodded. "If you say so."

Settling a gentle hand on the frail shoulder, Alex rose. "Let me get a bed ready for you."

Slipping out the door, he headed toward the waiting room. It might be best for Frank Macgregor to stay in his and Bryan's personal quarters during the day, so they could keep the front examination room open to see patients. It'd be hard to keep the back room warm enough, though. But he hated to infringe on Miriam's chamber. Especially since she still needed to rest throughout the day. Maybe she'd have a better idea.

"Miri—" His words died when he rounded the corner. Miriam. In the clutches of the big thug.

Rage boiled through him, and his fists crept to his right pocket. "Release her."

Baxter looked up, and surprise flashed in his eyes before an ugly sneer spread across his face. "Not fair you get all the fun, Doc."

Alex's hand closed over the ebony handle in his trouser pocket. Raising the revolver he kept there, he pulled the hammer and aimed the gun. The click filled the air, leaving behind a deadly silence. "Release. The lady."

Alex's gaze slipped to Miriam's face, and it was almost his undoing. Her wide green eyes shown fear, just above the grubby hand that covered her mouth. He couldn't let anything happen to her. *God, help me.*

He tightened his grip on the trigger, aiming for the man's head. "Let her go, Baxter. Miss Bryant is a patient here, and will be treated with the utmost respect and propriety. If you don't want a bullet in your thick skull, relcase the lady. Now."

Uncertainty flickered in the bully's eyes. Then he spat

a long dark stream, shoved Miriam away from him, and whirled toward the door. The glass window rattled as the door slammed.

Alex leaped forward and barely caught Miriam as she stumbled to balance herself with one good leg. She fell against his chest, and he gripped her tight. Miriam buried herself against him, and he wasn't sure which of them trembled more. He inhaled deeply, savoring the rich feel of her soft curls against his face. How had she become so important to him? More than any patient had ever been. So what to do with that knowledge? He let out a long breath. He could start by keeping her safe.

"I'm sorry, Miriam." His voice cracked on her name. "I never imagined that would happen."

She shuddered, taking in a long breath. Then she pulled back, her hands still resting on his chest. Teary green eyes met his, and Alex swallowed down the burn in his throat.

"It's not your fault, Alex. It was his." Her lips wobbled into a shaky smile. "Thank God you came to save me."

He wanted to take her face in his hands, to stroke her cheeks, touch those full lips. But his arms still supported her. He swallowed down his emotions. "Let's get you back to bed."

Chapter Thirteen

*M*iriam stood over the large pot on the stove to wring out the last of the bedding Mr. MacGregor used while he stayed at the clinic these last three days. The man had looked much better when he left this morning. He stood up straight now, had a little more meat on his frame, and didn't cough nearly so much. As she draped the blanket over a tall ladder-back chair, she kept one ear tuned to the male voices in the other room.

Alex would call if he needed her to assist, which was becoming more regular over the past few days. He'd not left her alone with a patient for even half a minute. Instead, he'd started allowing her to help with minor operations. He'd taught her how to prepare medicines, sanitize his supplies, anything that wouldn't tax her physically or strain her feminine sensibilities. As if she hadn't killed and plucked chickens, helped birth calves, and plenty of other gory things. Still, it was nice to be treated as both a lady, and partner. Able to really help make a difference. These last few days had been the most fulfilling she could remember.

The one piece of it all that tied a knot in her stomach was Alex. Not him exactly, but the worry lines that marred his forehead when she caught him looking at her. He hadn't left the clinic once since that ruffian attacked her. And as wonderful as it was to be working beside him, she didn't like being the cause of the worry he tried so hard to cover.

A knock sounded, and Miriam glanced over her shoulder at the open doorway.

Alex gave her one of his off-kilter grins that always sent her stomach into flips. "Do you mind if I bring Mister MacGrath in here? Looks like he'll need a tooth pulled. I could use your help if you're up for it." He eyed her, as if searching for any sign of doubt.

She flashed a pleasant smile while she dried her hands on her apron. "What all do you need?"

He stepped to the wash basin and poured clean water from the ewer. "The dental key and a dozen tiny bandage strips dipped in whiskey, about the size of your little finger."

Miriam adjusted the crutches under her arms, then swung to the cabinets. A dental key? Hopefully she could remember which tool that was.

Alex left the room, then returned with his patient trailing him. "Have a seat there on the table, Mister MacGrath, and we'll get you feeling better soon."

The man stood about Alex's height and had a thick shock of orange hair. That, along with the spray of freckles covering his nose and cheeks, confirmed what she'd suspected by his name alone. Irish or Scottish ancestry ran strong in his blood. Seemed there were a lot of people with that lineage in Butte these days.

"Aye, kill me now." With one side of his jaw swollen to almost twice the size of his other, the words came out sounding like "Ah, kew we na." But the brogue was still there. This man had to be a first generation immigrant.

After giving him something to help with the pain, Alex peered inside MacGrath's mouth. The man moaned.

She eyed Alex and their patient as she placed the tray of tools on the table where Alex could reach them.

Straightening, his gaze found Miriam's. "I'll need to pull the tooth. You may want to leave the room."

Miriam swallowed. If Alex could handle it, she could too. Right? She straightened her shoulders. "I'll be fine." *Lord, please let me be fine.*

Alex's lips pressed. Would he make her leave? He released a breath. "All right, but at least turn away for a minute."

Nodding, Miriam hobbled over to the stove. "Call if you need anything."

She busied herself drying the clean surgical instruments, but her mind assigned images to all the sounds coming from the examination table. Poor Mister MacGrath. His moans were pitiful. How bad must his pain be to bring such a strapping miner to this miserable state?

"Hold tight, man." Alex's murmured words barely registered before a mighty cry sounded.

Miriam whirled in time to see blood spurt from the man's mouth and Alex withdraw his hand and the dental key. He reached for the tiny bandages she'd prepared, then stuffed them inside MacGrath's mouth.

The man coughed, gasped, and then moaned again as he sunk back against the bed.

Miriam jerked a clean cloth from the washstand, soaked and wrung it quickly, then hobbled forward to wipe the crimson liquid dripping down their patient's chin and neck.

"There, there, Mister MacGrath. You'll be feeling

better in no time now." She kept her voice soothing, as she wiped the last remnants of sweat from his forehead.

The man's shoulders lay slack against the bed now, his head lolled to the side, eyelids drifting closed.

"The laudanum should be helping now, too. I'll let you rest a few minutes, then be back to check on you."

MacGrath only grunted.

Alex caught Miriam's eye and nodded toward the door. With a final glance at their resting patient, Miriam tucked her crutches under her arms and swung along behind him.

Once in the hallway, Alex stood uncertainly, hands out in front of him. "Do you, uh, mind if I use the washbasin in your room? My hands are bloody still."

"Of course."

She followed him into the chamber where she'd slept the last few weeks. Her eyes scanned the bed and table. Good thing she'd straightened it this morning. "What was wrong with Mister MacGrath's tooth?"

"Abscessed." Alex scrubbed the bar of lye soap over his blood-spattered hands and arms until it formed a pink lather. "Infection gets under the tooth. If it's not treated right away, the toxin becomes so bad the only way to cure it is to pull the tooth." He dipped both soapy arms into the basin of water. "I'll treat him for the infection when we go back in."

Miriam nodded, her mind playing through the possible remedies she knew about. Silver nitrate worked well to cure infections. Or maybe a garlic compress where the tooth had been.

Alex reached for the hand towel, turning as he dried his arms. Her eyes caught on the ripple of lean muscle under the dusting of dark hair on his forearms. She swallowed, forcing her gaze away from the attractive sight.

But her eyes seemed to wander of their own accord. Up, up. Until they landed in the rich depths of his chocolate gaze. A fire burned there, drawing her in.

Alex stepped closer, their bodies only a foot apart. His clean hand touched her cheek, its warmth sending a tingle all the way to her core.

"You're an amazing nurse." His words came out husky, and his breath played across her skin.

Was he going to kiss her? Every part of her craved it.

His eyes searched her face, his thumb caressing her cheekbone. His gaze landed on her lips, hovered there.

And then he sucked in a breath, and the transformation was instantaneous. He jerked his hand from her face, and stepped back, bumping into the wash stand. "I'm sorry." His gaze skittered to the floor, and he turned and strode out of the room, skirting a wide path around Miriam.

She could only stand there. What just happened? Had she done or said something to spook him? A long breath seeped from her lungs. Did he not feel the same sparks that shot through her when he was close?

Limping forward with her crutches, Miriam turned and sank onto her bed. Working so close to Alex, day after day…it was wonderful.

But how long could she do it before she lost her heart?

Alex held a tense breath as the razor blade scraped down his neck. After he pulled the sharp metal away, he exhaled, then eyed his face in the mirror. Strong features, fairly evenly proportioned. Although his nose was a bit larger than he'd like. Dad always said he had a real Irishman's nose. At least his brown hair was good and thick, although it needed a trim. Straight as it was, it hung down almost over his brows. He blew out a breath, ruffling the fray of bangs across his forehead.

"Goin' somewhere special?"

Alex jerked at the sound of Bryan's voice, and he spun to face his brother. "No, just cleanin' up."

Bryan's mouth twitched. "Maybe it's time you did go out."

Alex raised a brow. "Out where?"

"Anywhere. The café. The mercantile. Go inspect mines. Rent a horse from Jackson and ride up into the mountains." Bryan stopped lacing his boot, and turned his full attention on his brother. "You've got to get out, man. You haven't left the clinic since that lout attacked Miriam."

"I haven't needed to."

"You haven't had the nerve."

Heat rushed through Alex. "It has nothing to do with nerve."

Bryan cocked his head. "Then what is it?"

Alex tightened his jaw. He wasn't about to admit his feelings for the woman. Not with her still a patient in their clinic. "It's not safe to leave her alone."

"So today's my day to stay here. You're off the hook."

Off the hook? Like he was dying to ditch her the first chance he got?

Bryan threw up his hands. "Come on, Alex. No person in his right mind would stay holed up in this clinic day after day. Even Miriam's dying to get out of here." He hung his hands from his hips and stepped closer to Alex. "You have the chance, and I'm making you leave." He held up a single finger. "One hour. I don't care where you go or what you do, but you'll get out of my hair for one entire hour today. Got it?"

Something Bryan said wove its way back through Alex's mind. Miriam *had* said several times how much she wanted to see the mines. And after being cramped in this little clinic for almost four weeks now, she was probably dying to leave. But the idea was too crazy. Wasn't it? Would it strain her knee too much? Probably not any more than helping around the clinic. And mild exercise was beneficial for her body to heal now.

"Got it?"

His attention snapped back to Bryan, and he couldn't stop a grin from leaking onto his face. "Anything you say, big brother."

Miriam eyed Alex as she sat by the stove in the examination room, slicing bread for sandwiches. He'd had a twinkle in his eyes all morning, and now as he wrote notes in the patient journal from those they'd seen the day before, he actually whistled.

What had him in such a good mood? "You're especially chipper today."

He glanced up, eyes wide with innocence. "Me?"

"No, I meant your shadow."

His mouth tipped and he leaned over to peer at the dark spot on the floor by his chair. "What's that? You wanna go too?" He cocked his head as if listening to someone. "You think so?" He slanted a glance at Miriam. "I guess I can ask."

Miriam couldn't help a grin. What a goose he was.

Alex rose to his feet, jutted his chin like a pompous courier, and performed a deep bow. "Miss Bryant, my shadow and I extend an invitation for you to join us today for a tour of the mines."

What? Surely she hadn't heard right. "You mean…leave here?"

A dimple pressed in his left cheek. "If you can bear it."

If she'd been closer, she would have flung her arms around his neck. Instead, she clapped. "That would be…wonderful."

Luckily, he didn't make her wait long. Bryan joined them for sandwiches at lunchtime, then Alex left to hire a wagon from the livery.

As Miriam cleaned up the stove and filled a pot with beans to soak for dinner, Bryan came in with his arms full of some kind of fabric.

"Here's one of Alex's old coats. It'll be big on you, but better than nothing."

"But…where's my coat? Didn't I have it on when Gideon brought me down the mountain?" Now that she thought about it, the buckskin jacket wasn't with her few meager possessions tucked under the bed in her room.

"It was pretty much shredded. Not sure if Gideon took it with him or not, but you'll need this if you go."

That was for certain. It'd been bitterly cold when she'd stepped outside to empty her chamber pot earlier.

Bryan laid the coat on a chair back, and by the time Alex parked the wagon in front of the clinic, Miriam was snuggled inside the oversized wool jacket. It smelled of Alex. That minty freshness that drifted around him in the mornings after he'd shaved. And maybe a touch of the carbolic acid he used during surgeries. And there was something else, a unique aroma that was his alone. She breathed it in, and warmth spread through her.

Chapter Fourteen

"Who's ready for a grand tour?"

Miriam fastened the last button on the oversized coat as Alex's voice drifted from the front room. She tucked the crutches under her arms where the baggy sleeves hung low. "Coming."

Alex and Bryan both waited by the door as she hobbled into the front room.

"I've never seen two people so excited to look at a bunch of holes in the ground," Bryan grumbled as he handed Alex a thermos and a basket. He snapped his fingers. "Oh, I put some bricks in to heat. Let me get them for you."

As Bryan strode back down the hall, Alex's gaze took in Miriam. The corners of his eyes creased in a smile that made her stomach flutter. "That coat looks much better on you than it ever did on me."

She glanced down, trying to hide the warmth creeping into her face. The jacket bunched in thick creases around her arms, and the shoulder seams spread several inches wider than her own. "Thanks."

"Are we ready then? Your coach awaits, m'lady." He turned and extended his elbow. As if she were a real English lady and not an invalid who needed both hands to maneuver on the crutches.

As he held the door open for her, a glimmer flashed in his eyes. Excitement? Pleasure? She couldn't quite tell. But what would be so special for him about this outing? He had opportunities to drive through the countryside any day he pleased. Could it possibly be the company he looked forward to?

She stopped at the edge of the boardwalk and took in the sights and smells of the street. There wasn't much activity for an afternoon. Only a single wagon pulled by a pair of sorrel mules, and two men crossing over toward Ottawa Street. The frigid air nipped at her face in a way she hadn't ever fully appreciated before. Everything felt clean. Fresh. Not at all how she usually thought of Butte. But after being inside for weeks, even the dirty streets of this town made a welcome sight.

"The stairs might be tricky with the crutches. Okay if I carry you down?" Alex's voice rumbled close to her ear.

Miriam glanced down at the two steps to the ground. Surely she could manage something so simple.

He must have read her mind, though. "I'd rather you not take chances putting weight on that knee yet."

She glanced back at him and scrunched her nose. "All right."

He scooped her up, and the strength of his arms around her was more than all right. It was heaven. She rested her head on his shoulder, and the day would have been perfect if she could stay exactly like that.

He maneuvered the stairs and strode to the wagon,

placing her gently on the seat. Every part of her body resisted as she released her arms from his neck, and he pulled back. Stopping a few inches from her face, his gaze locked with hers. Miriam's chest tightened so she could barely breathe.

Alex seemed to be having the same trouble. Although his shortness of breath could be from carrying her weight. Was he going to kiss her? His face inched closer.

And then he pulled back, clearing his throat. His gaze fell to the wagon side, as his feet shuffled back.

Oh, why wouldn't he kiss her? Part of her wanted to grab his jacket front and drag his lips to hers. But the selfish, offended side of her would have enjoyed slapping the uncomfortable look right off his face.

The clinic door squeaked open, and Bryan marched out, carrying a crate of bricks, thick steam wafting from their clay surface. "I'll put these at your feet, then you can tuck this blanket around them to hold in the heat." He picked up a folded grey wool from over his arm.

While Bryan worked, Alex circled the wagon and climbed up beside her, leaving at least a foot of space between them.

Alex was quiet as they started off, and Miriam shot glances at his face. Had she offended him? He caught one of her peeks, and an emotion crossed his face like he was trying to shake off the gloom. A grin touched the corners of his mouth. "Feels good to be out, huh?"

There was the Alex she knew. Her face pulled into an answering smile as she tilted her head back to enjoy the limited sunshine on her face. "Wonderful."

They passed familiar buildings, and she couldn't help but crane her head for a better look in the windows of Lanyard's Dry Goods. What she wouldn't give for a hairbrush and a few other personal items.

"Maybe we can stop there on the way back through, if you're up to it." The rumble of Alex's voice brought her attention back to him. "Or if not, you can make a list for me to take to the clerk."

Warmth washed through Miriam, soothing away the tension in her shoulders. He was such a thoughtful man. One of the things that made him a good doctor. "Thanks."

The wagon hit a deep rut in the road, and Miriam braced her good leg to keep from falling off the seat. A knife of pain shot up from her left knee, even though she tried to keep that leg relaxed.

Alex eyed her. "Is the ride going to be too much?" He looked like he might turn back at a single word.

No way was she going back to the clinic early now that she'd finally escaped. Gripping the edge of the seat under the blanket, she flashed him a confident smile. "It's no problem at all."

As they passed through the outskirts of town, the buildings changed from false-front stores to rows of one- or two-room shanties. Several connected in clusters, building onto each other in order to share walls. Although some of them looked like the wind could blow straight through without ever hitting the wood siding.

The shacks became less frequent, and soon a tall wood tower appeared, like a church steeple, above the tops of a grove of leafless beech trees. Miriam eyed the turret, and as they rounded a curve in the road, the entire vertical structure came into view. She gasped. "What's that?"

"The headframe for the Travona mine."

The rectangular base, maybe ten feet by twenty, tapered on one side as it rose to a square tower. It must've been at least a hundred feet high. "What's it for? Where's the rest of the mine?" There weren't any other buildings or openings into the ground in sight.

Alex reined the horses in and set the brake on the wagon. "That's how the men get down to the ore, and how they bring it back up."

"Are there stairs inside that thing?"

"No, actually it's a pulley system that lowers them. From what I'm told, the early gold was discovered near the surface of the hill, so the miners built shafts with openings in the side of the mountain. But these silver veins are hundreds of feet down, so they use this main elevator to raise and lower things, then dig tunnels inside the ground to follow the ore."

A man that had been working at the base of the massive wood structure dropped the rope in his hands and strode their direction. "You got business here, mister?"

"Hello, sir. I'm Doc Alex, from the clinic." He extended his hand toward the man.

The miner stroked his beard and squinted at Alex under the brim of his cap. His gaze darted between the offered hand and Alex's face, then back to the extended hand. Finally, he took a cautious step forward and shook. "Don't need no doctor."

Alex kept his easy smile. "Glad to hear it. Miss Bryant was interested in seeing some of the mines."

The man's expression changed completely as his gaze took in Miriam, roaming quickly from her face down to the blanket covering her lap, and back up again. It wasn't an intrusive look, but more curious. Like a man who didn't see women very often and trying to refresh his memory.

"Hello, Mister..." She waited for his name.

"Halsten." He did an awkward little bow, and must have stepped on his own toes in the process for he almost fell headfirst.

Miriam bit her lower lip to hold in a smile. "So nice to meet you, Mister Halsten. I was just admiring the headframe." She motioned toward the towering wooden structure. "Do I understand correctly that it lowers the men down into the ground using pulleys? Do they hang from a rope, then?"

His mouth drew in a grim line. "Yes, ma'am. The pulleys raise and lower 'em, but they don't hang onto a rope. Leastways not the way you're meanin'. They ride up and down in a cage. Pack as many men in as we can, too. It's a long way down ta hundred feet underground."

"Is it awfully cold down there?" Miriam pulled her oversized jacket tighter as a breeze whipped against her.

"'Tis at first, but by the time the men get ta poundin' and carryin', they've worked up quite a sweat. When they come back up at the end of the day, it's a sight ta see. Wish you could be here for it, but you'll not wanna be hangin' round in this weather." He peered up at the overcast sky.

"What time do the men come up?" Miriam's gaze drifted back to the headframe, as if the men might come spilling out of the door at any moment.

The miner squinted as he still looked upward. "Two or three hours still."

After a few more minutes' conversation with the man, Alex gathered the reins. "We have a couple more mines to see, so we'd best head on. Good talkin' to you, Halsten."

The man tipped his cap as Alex clucked to the horses. When Miriam waved to the miner, his mouth spread into a wide gap-tooth grin that transformed his face. She couldn't help a chuckle.

The Alice and the Original mines were similar to the Travona. Each headframe was a site to behold. At the

Original, they dismounted from the wagon, and Miriam hobbled on her crutches over to the base of the structure. Every miner they met was more than eager to answer questions and tell his own stories of operating the pulleys or digging out the underground shafts. No matter the speaker, each tale reinforced in Miriam's mind what miserable life mining must be. Underground all day, rarely seeing daylight. Her own soul would shrivel up and die under such conditions. How did the men endure it?

When they drove away from the Original, Alex turned the wagon back onto the road the way they'd come. Miriam pulled the coat he'd loaned her even tighter around herself, and hunkered down like a turtle in a shell. She clamped her jaw against the chattering of her teeth. What she wouldn't give for her buckskin jacket, and her fur hat and gloves.

"Scoot closer and we can share body heat." Alex spoke above the whistle of the wind that had whipped up.

She was too miserable to worry about whether that was proper or not. Every muscle in her body ached from the cold, especially her left knee. Scooting over, she closed the gap on the seat between them, and reached to thread her hand through his elbow. He raised his arm though, and slipped it behind her, encircling her shoulders and pulling her close to his side. His warmth penetrated quickly, and Miriam burrowed deeper. Tucked under his wing, her teeth soon stopped chattering. She matched her breathing to the steady intake of his.

They drove for a while. How long, she couldn't have said. Alex's warmth permeated every part of her upper body. Her toes were numb, but that didn't matter a whit. The air took on that dusky feel when the sun sinks lower on an overcast day. Too bad they couldn't see a beautiful sunset, with pinks and blues and oranges. That would have been the perfect close to a wonderful afternoon.

"We'll drive right by the Travona." Alex's voice rumbled in her ear. Deep, yet soft. Intimate. "I know it's cold, but I was hoping you would get to see the miners come out of the shaft. Are you up for a quick stop?"

She looked up to meet his gaze. Their faces mere inches apart. "Yes, I'm fine." But she was better than fine. Close enough to touch his face with her breath. If she could have breathed. It would be so easy to brush his cheek with her lips. Her gaze fell to his mouth. But what would he think? No lady would initiate such a thing.

Tucking her head back against his side, she released a long shuddering breath. Alex's arm tightened around her, pulling her even closer into him. But it was several minutes before his steady breathing raised his chest against her shoulder.

When they reined in again in front of the Travona headframe, Mr. Halsten stuck his head out of the open door at the base. "Didn't expect to see you'uns back. Yer just in time, though. We're fixin' to bring up a cage full o' miners."

Miriam sat straighter, anticipation warming her insides. A man's shout ricocheted inside the wooden structure. An awful squeak signaled the first turn of the gears, then grinding noises kept up a steady purr. Several minutes passed, with no change in the regular turning of the gears.

Letting out a huff, Miriam sank against Alex's side. "Do you think they're coming?"

A chuckle reverberated in his chest. "Patience. It takes a while to travel up a hundred feet."

Chapter Fifteen

It must have been a quarter hour later when Miriam heard male voices inside the headframe. Shouts mostly, one or two sharp words called over the noise of the metal. With another ear-piercing squeal, the gears ground to a halt, leaving behind a silence so eerie it raised goose bumps on Miriam's arms.

A white cloud drifted from the opening. Miriam blinked. Men walked inside the hazy fog. The dark movement of their boots was visible at the bottom, and as the cloud cleared, caps and dark faces appeared at the top.

"Is that...steam?" She couldn't take her eyes from the uncanny sight.

"Yep. The men have worked up such a sweat underground, when they reach the cold air at the surface, their clothes freeze stiff. The steam is the heat from their bodies melting their frozen clothing."

The miners trudged toward the road, limited words spoken between them. Every few seconds, one of them would cough. Weariness weighed down every step they took, pressing down broad shoulders so they looked like a defeated lot of men. Miriam's heart squeezed and tears burned the backs of her eyes. Everything in her cried out to help these men, but what could she do? They'd put in a hard day's work, but it was likely the same thing they did every day. Week after week.

That horrible squeal sounded again, sending Miriam's heart into double time at the suddenness of it.

"The cage is going down to bring up another load of miners. Shall we head back now?" Alex's thumb rubbed her arm through the coat.

"All right." Miriam swallowed down the lump in her throat.

As they drove, the image of those faces, so soot-streaked they were almost black, played over and over in her mind. "Alex."

"Hmm..." His chin rested on her hair for just a moment.

"Why would men keep working in the mines? It looks like a terrible way to live. Down in the ground all day, not coming to the surface until dark. So exhausted they can barely walk home. Why don't they find other jobs?"

Alex was quiet for so long, she almost looked up to make sure he was awake. At last he spoke. "For most of them, it's the only work they know how to do. They're not skilled at a trade, like blacksmithing or carpentry. A lot of them came over from Ireland. Some during the potato famine years back. There's nothing else for them to do. In the cities, they would starve to death." He stopped speaking, and his shoulders lifted as he inhaled a deep breath. "It's an awful life."

With a flash of awareness, Miriam saw Alex as a boy in that life. He was Irish. He'd come from a big city. Had his family almost starved to death? But his father was skilled, right? Hadn't Alex said he was an apothecary? Did that mean Alex's life had been different than so many of his countrymen? She didn't dare ask. How did one go about inquiring if a man came from a poor family? No, his speech was cultured, not the rough working-man brogue of the miners she'd met. And hadn't he and Bryan both gone to a prestigious college in Canada?

A single phrase came back to her then. Something Pa used to say when she was a girl. *But for the grace of God go I.* Heart raised in silent prayer. *Lord, thank You that Your mercies are new every day.*

Soon, they rolled into the outskirts of town. Miriam had expected to pass the miners on the road who they saw leaving the Travona, but as she eyed the men milling around the shanties, none looked familiar. Although with the miners' faces blackened, there was a chance she wouldn't recognize them.

"Where are the men we saw leave the mine?" She sat up straighter, putting a few inches between her and Alex. Now that they were in town, propriety was more important.

Alex must have sensed her concern, because he pulled his arm out from behind her, gripping the reins with both hands. "There are trails all through the woods around Butte. I imagine they took a shortcut home. Men on foot outside of town can sometimes get to a place twice as quick as a man in a wagon that has to stay on the road."

By the time Alex reined the wagon to a stop in front of the clinic, Miriam's teeth chattered again, and she hunkered down inside her coat.

"Let me come around." Alex set the brake and jumped from the wagon. After he'd jogged to Miriam's side, he handed her the walking sticks, then scooped her in his arms, and carried her up the steps. His warmth was heavenly, and she fought the urge to burrow into his chest.

Alex planted her gently on the boardwalk, and Miriam leaned against him until she had the sticks firmly planted under her arms.

"Are you sure you can walk?" He hadn't taken his arm from her waist.

Miriam forced a smile through her chattering teeth. "Yes."

"Let's get you inside then."

Miriam blinked open her eyes and stretched, turning over to gauge the time by how much light seeped through the window. Bright sunlight streamed through the dingy glass.

She bolted upright. How late had she slept? This lady of leisure stuff was making her soft. Too soft.

Hurrying through her toilette, she scrubbed her face in the frigid water from the ewer, wiped her teeth with a clean rag, and finger-combed her hair before refastening the braid.

In the next room, the scrape of chair legs sounded, along with the low hum of male voices. What must the men think of her? And she'd promised to take care of all the meals from now on. If they hadn't given up on her and started breakfast themselves, the Donaghue brothers were surely starving by now.

Fitting the crutches under her arms, she hobbled through her door and followed the voices to the examination room that also served as kitchen and eating area.

Alex stood at the stove, scrubbing a bowl over a pot of water. His face brightened when he saw her in the doorway. "G'mornin'."

"Morning." Miriam swung forward. "Let me take care of that. Sorry I'm so late this morning."

She stopped at the stove and nudged Alex aside with her elbow. He didn't budge, but nodded toward the table where Bryan sat. "I left a plate of food for you." He wrinkled his nose. "Such as it is."

"Alex's specialty. Rubber eggs and burnt bacon." Bryan leaned back in his chair, long legs stretched in front of him, with a mug of coffee in both hands.

Miriam nibbled her lower lip as she turned back to Alex. "Are you sure?"

A dimple pressed into his left cheek. "Am I sure the bacon's burned? 'Fraid so. I went to pump more water and the fire was hotter than I figured. Go ahead and eat."

That grin always melted her insides. "All right. Thanks."

But as she hobbled to the chair and lowered herself into it, her stomach tightened so much she likely wouldn't be able to eat anything. It was time she stopped imposing on these men. She'd be forever grateful for their care and kindness, and maybe she could still come and help at the clinic to work off her debt to them. But they certainly didn't need to worry about her as a houseguest. And that's what she'd become.

Miriam picked at the food on her plate, forcing a weak smile when Bryan slid a cup of coffee in front of her. The eggs shone golden, but were cold and rubbery as Bryan had joked. With all of Alex's skill as a doctor, he shouldn't have to worry about cooking when she was perfectly capable.

She inhaled a deep breath, then looked up. Her gaze skittered between the two brothers. "Do you think my injuries are healed enough for me to move to the boarding house?"

Metal clanged at the stove, followed by a splash from the pan. Alex mumbled something under his breath and grabbed his right hand with his other.

"Are you okay?" Miriam started to her feet, but he waved her away.

He still kept his right hand against his shirt. "I'm fine." But he almost snarled the words. How badly was he injured?

Miriam hesitated, her hand poised on the table to help her rise. He must have burned his hand when he dropped the mug in the pot of hot water. Should she help him tend to it? She knew as well as anyone how bad a burn could hurt. But Bryan was a doctor, so he would be worried if Alex was really hurt. Right?

Bryan cleared his throat, drawing Miriam's attention. "I suppose we'd need to do an examination to make sure. If everything looks okay, you should be fine to move."

Miriam blinked. It took several seconds before she realized he was answering her question.

She flicked a glance at Alex, but his back faced them as he bent over the firebox. Turning to Bryan, she inhaled a deep breath. "When do you want to do the examination?"

He nodded toward her food. "Finish breakfast, then we'll take a look."

A half hour later, Miriam settled herself on the examination table, while Bryan and Alex gathered clean water and supplies. Her stomach twisted in a hundred knots, and her shoulders ached from the tension building in her muscles.

Not only did her next steps depend on the outcome of

this examination, but things were different now. Her relationship with these men had become more than that of a patient and doctors. Bryan reminded her of Gideon more every day, with his dry humor and penchant to hoard words. Like each one cost him half a day's work.

And Alex. Butterflies flitted in her stomach even now as she thought of him. What did that mean? She was attracted to him, no doubt. Who wouldn't be, with the way he lit up a room just by walking into it? The way he made each person feel they were special? When really...Alex was the special one. Miriam's chest squeezed at the thought. Could she be falling in love with him?

Boot thuds in the hall brought a swift end to that thought.

"All right, let's have a look at that knee." Bryan slipped his surgery smock over his head as he stepped forward.

Alex crossed the room toward the washbasin without a word. Was he angry with her? Now that she thought about it, he hadn't given her more than a word or a nod since she sat down to breakfast.

After she inched her hem up to reveal the splinted knee, Bryan began unwrapping the stiff leather splint. A soft scrape of wood behind her pulled Miriam's focus from his work.

Alex placed a chair at her shoulder and settled into it. The tension eased out of her muscles. Having him near was like snuggling under a warm quilt on a cold winter morning. She sent him a smile to try to convey her thanks.

Just as her gaze connected with his, a knife of pain shot from her knee to her hip. Miriam bit hard on her lip to keep from crying out.

Alex's hand slid into hers, encircling her palm with

his long fingers. She squeezed it as another jab radiated through her thigh.

He glanced at where Bryan worked, then his gaze came back to find her eyes. "He almost has it unwrapped." His expression was a mixture of compassion and a hint of her own pain. As if he were trying to take it on himself.

She locked her focus in Alex's amber gaze, forcing aside the throbbing that rippled with every touch of Bryan's surgical probe.

"You're doing great," Alex murmured, as his thumb stroked the back of her hand.

Time seemed to stand still, until Bryan finally glanced up from where he'd bent over her knee. "Everything's looking good. I'll wrap the knee with a softer splint this time. The exercises are helping, and it's good you're up and moving on crutches now." He looked to Alex. "You wanna examine the arm while I wrap this back up?"

Alex nodded, then pulled his hand from hers with a soft smile. He carried his chair to her other side, and organized a few supplies on the edge of the bed.

Miriam watched his movements as she tried to ignore Bryan's ministrations to her knee.

Alex's touch was so gentle, as he cut the knot holding the bandage around her wrist, then carefully unwrapped it. The burn smarted when the air hit it, but only for a moment. Alex squinted as he examined all sides of her forearm and the back of her hand. "Looks good. The blisters didn't pop, and they're almost completely gone." He glanced up at her. "It should be fine to leave it unwrapped now. Just be careful it doesn't get dirty, and put this salve on twice a day."

Miriam released the breath she hadn't realized she'd been holding. "Maybe I can keep from getting hurt this time."

A smile touched Alex's mouth as he spread the salve over the mottled red skin on her arm.

Miriam swallowed. "So does this mean I can move to the boarding house?"

The smile disappeared from Alex's lips, replaced by a grim line. But he didn't answer.

Bryan spoke up. "I think that should be fine. As long as you're careful, and we can make arrangements for someone to check in on you." His brows lowered. "I don't recommend you leave town though."

Miriam forced her lips into a smile. "That's not a problem. The mountain trail must not be passable yet, or Gideon would have come."

While Bryan finished her leg, Alex gathered the leftover supplies and dirty bandages. He didn't speak a word, and wouldn't meet her gaze. A far cry from his earnest support a few minutes before. What had she done to upset him? Wouldn't he be glad to have her out from underfoot?

She watched his rigid shoulders as he put away the unused bandage in the cabinet, laid the metal instruments they'd employed in the to-be-cleaned bin, and tossed the soiled cloths in the wash stack. With everything put away, he strode to the doorway and disappeared. Without a word. No easy smile. No cheery comments to brighten her mood or ease her discomfort.

"He'll be all right."

Miriam's gaze shot to Bryan's face. His eyes flickered a sad smile. Could she ask what was wrong with Alex? She couldn't quite bring herself to.

But when she had a moment, she'd talk to Alex herself.

Chapter Sixteen

*M*iriam blinked. Where was she? Another blink brought her surroundings into focus. With a yawn, she sat up. Why was she sleeping in the middle of the day? She pulled her shoulders into a stretch, then leaned back against the wall at the head of the bed.

She'd had a cup of willow tea to help with the pain after her examination, and it must have put her to sleep. Pushing aside the blankets, she used her hands to lift her bad leg to the cold floor. How long had she slept? After being so late waking this morning, and now a nap in the middle of the day, these doctors probably wrote her off as useless. And Miriam Bryant may be a lot of things, but useless was not one of them.

In the small mirror Alex had set up for her, Miriam frowned at her appearance. She'd need to rebraid her hair. For the second time today. As her fingers worked through the task, her mind wandered to the morning's events when she'd announced her plans to move. Alex had been so strange. She needed to talk with him and find out what she'd done to offend him. Maybe over lunch, or in between patients if it was a slow day.

She stilled her movements to listen. No voices drifted through the walls. It didn't sound like Alex was with anyone at the moment. Her fingers fumbled with the ribbon. Why was she shaking? Was it so hard to talk to Alex? Silly girl. He was the easiest man she'd ever conversed with.

Grabbing the crutches, she hobbled toward the hall. As she entered the main examination room, Alex glanced up from the chair by the desk. He'd been reading a book, his legs propped on the wooden desk.

His face formed a smile when he saw her, but it didn't quite reach his eyes. "There's coffee on the stove, and I sliced bread, cheese, and beef for sandwiches. Are you hungry?" Dropping his legs to the floor, he started to rise.

"Don't get up. Please." She'd inconvenienced him enough already. "I just need coffee right now. I'll get it." It was time she cared for herself.

She filled the cup half full so it didn't spill while she hobbled, and limped to sit in the chair beside the desk.

Alex dropped his attention back to the book. Should she interrupt him? If she'd offended him, she needed to make it right.

Miriam cleared her throat. "Alex?"

He glanced up, his brown eyes wary. "Yes?"

"Um, what are you reading?" *Chicken.*

He lifted the book so she could see its cover. "*Medical Flora of the United States.*"

"Interesting." She moistened her lips. "Have I, um, done something to offend you?"

His gaze shot to her face, but he didn't answer. Just sat there, as if debating what to say. Was whatever she'd done so bad?

He rose and walked to the window, staring out at a passing wagon and the mountain range beyond. At last, he spoke. "Bryan stopped by Watson's Boarding House. They'll have a room ready for you tomorrow."

That didn't answer her question. Did it? Something about her presence—or leaving—had upset him. Did he think her ungrateful?

Placing her coffee on the desk, she pushed to her feet, choosing her words carefully. "Alex, I can't tell you how much I appreciate everything you've both done. Everything *you've* done. I'd like to keep helping in the clinic, if I can. That is…" She crossed her arms over her chest. "If I would be a help, and not get in the way."

He waved toward the stove. "You're always a help. Everything you do around here is a breath of fresh air. Your cooking is fit for royalty compared to mine." Alex spun to face her. "Patients love you, and when you're helping me with a procedure, you think two steps ahead of me."

He strode back across the room and placed his hands on her upper arms. The warmth of his touch seared through her sleeves. "I love having you here. I lo—" He stopped himself before finishing the sentence, dropping his arms to his sides. What had he been about to say?

"I don't want you to overdo it, though. Come when you can, but don't push yourself." His forehead puckered. "I'm not sure I want you coming by yourself, though. The sidewalks are still icy, and those crutches could be dangerous outside. Why don't you wait for me to come walk with you? Or I could bring you in the wagon."

Miriam reached for both of Alex's wrists, sliding her hands down until they fit in his. "I'll be fine. Thanks to your skills, my knee's getting better every day. I'm trying to make this easier on you, not harder."

He loosened one hand and reached up to finger a curl that had escaped her braid. When his gaze found hers, the amber flecks darkened to a rich chocolate. "I understand. You're the kindest woman I've ever known."

His hand cradled her cheek, and Miriam couldn't help but lean into the touch. His eyes wandered to her face, coming to rest on her lips. She could feel his gaze. Like a warm breath.

And then it *was* his breath. Her eyes drifted closed as his lips touched hers.

Sweet molasses. Like nothing she'd ever experienced.

As Alex's lips made contact with hers, a spark traveled all the way to his core.

By jingo, she was sweet.

He deepened the kiss, his senses filling with every part of her. The softness of her lips, the hint of coffee lacing her breath. The intensity of her response. He pressed harder, slipping a hand to her back and pulling her closer.

She stumbled, and the jolt cracked the trance of her kiss. *What was he doing?* Alex pulled back, sliding his arms to her shoulders. As much to steady himself as her.

He struggled to catch his breath, not able to meet her gaze. "I'm sorry." He had to get out of there. His body still raged with the desire to pull her close again.

"I'm sorry, I—" But he had no words to describe what he was feeling. Wasn't even sure himself. This woman may be all he'd ever dreamed of, but she was his patient. *Get out of there.*

Jerking his hands from her, he turned and strode out

the door.

Miriam fumbled for the arms of the chair behind her, then sank into its seat. What just happened? The amazing effects of the kiss still lingered inside her. She pressed two fingers to her lips.

But the look in his eyes when he'd pulled away? Pure torture.

Had it been so bad for him? She'd never kissed a man before. Had no idea it was so...magical. But maybe she'd done it all wrong.

It sure hadn't felt wrong, though.

Miriam leaned on her crutches by the front door as she fastened the buttons spanning the front of Alex's borrowed coat. Both brothers insisted on walking with her to the boarding house. That was probably a good thing, as Alex had been stiff and formal since their kiss the day before. He seemed to take pains not to be alone with her. And when they were in the same room with Bryan or a patient, he never made eye contact. When he spoke to her, red usually crept into his face and ears.

If the kiss had been so bad, why couldn't he just forget it? Maybe she should apologize. But for what? For being a bad kisser? That would be awkward, and then some. At least she wouldn't be sleeping at the clinic anymore, which would lessen their chances of being alone together.

"All set?" Bryan strode into the front room with her meager bundle of possessions tucked under his arm. Alex appeared behind him, doctor's bag in hand.

She raised a questioning gaze on them both. "Are you going on calls after you drop me at the boarding house?"

"Never know when we'll need it. Like to be prepared with both of us out." Alex didn't meet her gaze, but strode around his brother to open the front door.

Bryan gave her a good-natured smile, and touched her elbow. "Ready when you are."

It was a long, silent walk down the block, across the street, and around the corner to Watson's. A little sun poked through the clouds, but the breeze that whipped up stung bitter cold. The coat helped, but she'd need to purchase one, or make her own, soon. She couldn't keep depending on Alex.

Bryan had secured a room for her on the first floor. A blessing, since stairs were still tricky with her crutches. Mrs. Watson led them to the room—second door on the left—and motioned for Miriam to precede her into the small chamber. The men stayed in the hallway.

"You just open your door an' call if you need anything, dearie. Mister Watson an' I stay at the other end of the hall, so I'll be listenin' for you." She was a petite woman, with curly brown hair cut short so it framed her heart-shaped face. Her puffy cheeks seemed to keep a constant rosy hue.

"Thank you." Miriam reached for the bundle from Bryan.

"Let me get that, hon." Mrs. Watson stepped in front of her to take it, then dropped the package on the bed. "I don't usually cook meals since the café's right next door." She paused, tilting her head at Miriam. "If I need to have something delivered, though..."

"Oh, no. I'll be helping at the clinic still, so I'll take most of my meals there." She shot a gaze at the men. Bryan eyed her with raised brows, but Alex only stared at his boot as it scuffed the floor. Had Alex not shared that news with his brother?

"I'll leave you be then." Mrs. Watson eyed the men, as if she weren't sure if she should leave Miriam alone with them.

"Thank you, Mrs. Watson. I appreciate all your help." Miriam gave the woman a smile and was rewarded with a pat on the shoulder.

"Any time, dearie. You just call."

The brothers murmured their thanks as she strode past. Bryan glanced around the room again. "You need anything to get settled?"

Miriam nibbled her lip. She needed more than she cared to say in front of male ears. "I do need a few things from the mercantile. Is there any way I could give you a list for the next time one of you go there? You can put it on Gideon's tab."

Bryan nodded. "Of course. If you write it now, we'll get it today." She couldn't see Alex's face where he stood, almost behind his brother.

Miriam glanced at the paper and charcoal on the nightstand. "I'll be quicker than a rifle shot."

After jotting down everything she could think of—from a comb to wool material and thread for a new cape—she swung on the crutches to the door. Neither man had dared step foot over the threshold.

"You can just give this to the clerk to gather." *Please.* The last thing she wanted was for these men to select her toiletries.

Alex stepped forward, reaching for the paper. "I'll stop back by with the supplies around lunchtime." He didn't quite meet her gaze, but it was the first time he'd spoken without being forced since the kiss.

"Thank you."

He was an idiot.

Alex pounded the words in his head as his boots slapped the wooden sidewalk. How could he have crossed the line with Miriam like that? Kissed her. While she was a patient under his care. He ground his fingertips into his palms.

He had to apologize. Had to clear the air between them. Promise it wouldn't happen again. And then he had to make sure it didn't...

Breathing in a deep breath, he straightened his shoulders. When he brought her supplies from the mercantile, they would talk.

"Ya know, she likes you." Bryan elbowed his side.

Alex scowled. "She's a patient, Bryan."

His brother waited a few moments before answering. "True. But she won't always be. Give it time. Don't close any doors."

Alex clenched his jaw. *Don't close any doors?* How could he see Miriam every day—work alongside her and experience her kindness and intelligence, not to mention her good cooking—without craving her as more in his life? The only way he could do it was by slamming that door shut and boarding it up. She was OFF LIMITS. No touching. Business only.

Now to explain it to her in a way that didn't break her heart. Because that would be his undoing.

Chapter Seventeen

*W*hen the knock sounded on Miriam's door, she slipped the ribbon in *Emma* to mark her page. "Coming."

Holding in a groan, she pushed off the bed and fit a crutch under her left arm. She was getting good at maneuvering with a single walking stick in these small spaces. Before she opened the door, Miriam brushed loose curls back from her face, then smoothed her skirt. Would Alex be in a better mood this time? Inhaling a deep breath, she grasped the handle.

The aroma of baked chicken and potatoes hit her first, even before she saw the large box piled high enough to hide the person carrying it. The crate shifted, and Alex's head peered around it. "Hungry?"

"I wasn't until I smelled that." She hobbled out of the way. "Bring it on in."

As he lowered his load to the floor, Miriam peered over his shoulder and realized it was two crates stacked. "I don't remember baked chicken on my list."

He lifted covered plates, jars, and utensils from the

top crate and placed them on the dresser. "Figured you'd be settling in today, so you wouldn't make it to the clinic. And I wasn't sure you'd go to the café yourself." He shot her a look, his mouth quirked.

"I would if I got hungry enough." She limped to the dresser and lifted the cloth off a plate. The warm, savory aroma blasted her face. "Oh, that's heavenly."

That familiar twinkle sparkled in his eye. "Enjoy. There should be enough for dinner too." Rising, he lifted the crate that was still half full of food and settled it under one arm.

"Aren't you going to stay and eat with me?" Miriam's heart sank as she realized his intent.

Alex glanced down at the wood box he held. "I need to get back to the clinic. Left it closed too long already."

He paused, his brow furrowing, eyes still staring at the cloth covering in the crate. Then he raised his head and met Miriam's gaze squarely. The beat in her chest quickened.

"Miriam, I'm sorry about yesterday. I shouldn't have…done that." His gaze dropped to the floor, and red seeped into his cheeks. "I mean…you're a patient and I don't want you to be uncomfortable. I won't let it happen again."

Miriam's mind spun. Was he saying he'd stopped kissing her because she was under his medical care? Suddenly, it was more important that she make certain of that, than take her next breath. She squared her shoulders. "So you didn't hate the kiss?"

His head jerked up, brown eyes widening. "Hate it? No." His eyes darkened to chocolate, and the shadow of a smile touched his mouth. "A far opposite from hate."

And then he blinked, the red in his cheeks deepening to crimson. "But I shouldn't have done it. I'm sorry. It won't happen again." With a bow, his voice slipped into the Irish brogue. "I'll endeavor to be the perfect gentleman doctor, deserving of a fine lady patient such as yourself."

Dipping his chin, he turned and glanced toward the door. "I need to go now. I'll check on you in the morning. Is there anything else you need?"

No matter how she tried to hold it back, a smile forced its way onto Miriam's face. It didn't matter, though. He wasn't looking at her as he edged to the door. "This is more than enough. Thank you."

With one final look and a nod, Alex walked out the door, closing it behind him.

Alex plunged the pen into its inkwell and slumped against the back of his chair with a sigh. What a day. After he'd left Miriam at lunchtime, there'd been a steady stream of patients into the office. At times, two or three waiting for him. And as the day progressed, the clinic grew lonelier by the minute. Too many memories of Miriam, everywhere he turned.

Even his patients wouldn't let him forget about her. Mrs. Malmgren had stepped in the front door, ignored his greeting, and cocked her head like she was listening for raindrops. Then she waved her cane at him, her blind eyes wide. "Where's that pretty gal you were doctorin' on? You didn't run her off, did ya?"

Alex had pasted a smile on his face, so maybe it would come through his voice. "No, ma'am. She's doing much better and staying at the boarding house now."

A ship could have drowned in the frown lines covering her face. "Don't you lose her, Alex Donaghue."

The smile was a little easier this time, as he reached forward to take her elbow. One couldn't get upset with this spunky old woman. "Yes, ma'am. Come on back and we'll see how you're doing today."

She jerked her arm from his grasp. "Don't patronize me. You boys've moved too far away from your mama. Somebody's gotta do the job."

Alex couldn't help but smile at the memory of the sassy lady. But now his patients were all gone, leaving him alone. It'd been dark for at least an hour, and Bryan still wasn't back from his rounds.

At last, the front door opened in the next room, allowing the sound of the wind to howl in, until the click of the door shut it out. Alex leaped to his feet and strode to meet his brother. "It's about time you're back. Everything all right?"

Bryan stood just inside the room as he shucked his gloves first, then his coat. "Not exactly."

Alex's focus jerked to the tight expression on Bryan's face. "What's wrong?"

He let out a long breath. "Frank MacGregor died."

Every muscle in Alex's body went taut.

"He didn't show up for work this morning, so they sent a man to his shack."

Alex's throat worked, but no sound came out.

Bryan met his gaze. "He was in a bad way, Alex. You knew as well as I did he might not make it."

Alex stumbled back, bumped into the corner next to the hallway wall, and clung hard to the door post. "But he seemed so much better when he left here. He wasn't coughing blood anymore, and his breathing was easier."

Bryan's lips pinched. "His neighbor said his cough got worse after his first night home. Could hear him coughing all night through the walls."

"Then why didn't he come back to the clinic?"

Bryan gripped his shoulder, the volume in his voice dropping. "I don't know. You did the best you could, but I guess he knew he was dying. We can't fight God when a man's time comes."

Alex's jaw clenched. Can't fight God? Why didn't God help these people? The ache in his chest that had grown through the afternoon without Miriam was strong enough now to double him over. He'd failed again.

Alex squared his shoulders as he stood in front of Miriam's door at the boarding house. Would she be up yet? Maybe she wasn't planning to come to the clinic today. He didn't want her to think he needed her there. No matter how much that was true.

Inhaling a deep breath, he raised his knuckles and tapped on the wooden door.

Rustling sounded inside, then several soft thuds, and finally a muffled, "You can open it."

Alex reached for the wood knob and slowly twisted it. As he pushed the door open, Miriam stood at the foot of her bed, crutches under both arms. She was more beautiful than he'd ever seen her.

Her honey-blonde curls were pulled up into a coif that perfectly accented her elegant cheekbones. His eyes fell to the creamy skin of her slender neck. Everything about her was stunning.

"Good morning."

He swallowed, trying to summon liquid into his dry

mouth.

"I'm ready." She hobbled forward.

"Ready?" He had to pull himself together.

She stopped a few feet from him. Her delicate brown brows arched and a smile played on her lips. "To go to the clinic."

He forced his gaze from her lips and focused on her eyes. A brownish green this morning, close to the olive color of her skirt. The skirt he'd picked out for her. "Oh. All right."

She still stood there, brows raised and watching him as if waiting.

Alex tore his gaze from Miriam and looked around. Was she waiting on him?

"Well, let's go then."

Right. Alex jumped to the side, then motioned toward the hall with a flourish. "After you, m'lady."

"Oh, I forgot my jacket. I mean, your jacket." She turned to retrieve the coat laying on the bed.

"I'll get it." He almost tripped over his feet getting into the room. *Smooth, Donaghue. Get a handle on yourself.*

When they stepped out the front door, Alex took a deep breath of the biting air. A fresh layer of snow had fallen in the night. Powdery and clean still, except for the single track that had formed in the middle of the street.

"Watch out for ice." He gripped Miriam's arm as she maneuvered the two stairs to the road so they could cross.

"Thanks." Her brow puckered as she carefully placed the crutches with each step. "Thanks for coming to get me this morning. You won't have to do it every day though. I should be fine after this first time."

A smile tugged at his mouth. Such a strong-willed lass.

As the clinic came into view ahead, the gloom that

hovered all night settled again over Alex's shoulders. Another patient. Lost. What was he doing wrong?

"Do you want to talk about it?" Miriam's voice was so soft, he almost didn't hear her over the breeze.

"Talk about what?" Had she sensed something wrong? Or did she want to discuss their conversation yesterday.

She cut him a glance. "Whatever's worrying you."

Alex let out a long breath. How could she read him so well? And she wanted him to talk about it? But something deep inside him did want to confide in her. Not that she could do anything about it. But still...

"Frank MacGregor died."

Her quick inhale was loud enough to hear over the wind. "No. He was getting better."

Alex kept his focus planted on the boardwalk ahead of them. "Appears he worsened not long after he left us."

"Alex, I'm so sorry." The grief in her words made him stop and turn to look at her.

Miriam touched his arm, and the pressure sank through his wool coat. Like a balm to his soul.

A rush of something burned the back of his eyes, but Miriam turned and continued hobbling down the sidewalk. He swallowed to collect himself.

"Do you think the pneumonia came back? Or was there something more?"

That was the question, wasn't it? Alex scrubbed a hand through his hair. "I don't know. The pneumonia seemed to be out of his lungs. I wonder if there's something in the mine that could have triggered the relapse." He sighed. "I guess we'll never know for sure."

They reached the clinic door, and he opened it for her to enter.

"Oh, warmth." She moved straight for the examination room where he'd loaded the stove box with wood. Beside the stove, she propped her crutches against the wall and slipped her coat off. "So what can I do first?"

"A garlic poultice on your feet should help." Alex handed his stethoscope to Miriam as he stepped away from Mrs. Mason—or Aunt Pearl as she was better known.

Aunt Pearl wrinkled her nose. "I'll stink worse'n a skunk in the outhouse."

Alex chuckled. "If you put it on while you're sleeping and then wash it off in the morning, you shouldn't smell a thing that day."

Out of the corner of his eye, Alex saw Miriam tying garlic cloves in a piece of cloth. Always right in step with him.

A crash sounded in the front room, accompanied by male shouts and boot thuds. "Doc!"

Alex jumped to his feet and ran toward the sounds. When he rounded the corner, three men were coming in the front door. The middle one had been badly beaten and was supported by a fellow on either side. It took several seconds before Alex's mind caught up with what his eyes took in.

The battered man was Bryan.

Chapter Eighteen

"Bring him in here." Miriam motioned for the men to help Bryan to the examination room.

Her words seemed to spur Alex into action, although his face paled as white as the painted fence around the churchyard.

"Lands," Aunt Pearl breathed as the men shuffled through with Bryan. "You take care of him, an' I'll send some broth over with one of the girls."

Miriam shot her a grim look. "Thanks." Then she followed the men into the room.

They'd need warm water to start with. There was so much blood on Bryan's face, it was hard to see the damage. Although one of his eyes had already swollen almost shut.

Alex examined his brother while she brought in the wash basin and a clean cloth.

"I'll need a suture needle and thread."

Miriam hobbled to the cabinets to gather supplies. Arnica would help with the swelling. And a cold compress of snow for that eye. She carried the materials back to the bedside table.

"I'm fine," Bryan mumbled, pushing Alex's hand away. "Just need rest and willow tea for this bloody headache."

Willow tea. Why hadn't she thought of that? Miriam limped to the stove and poured clean water in the empty pot.

"How did this happen, Bryan?" Alex's voice held a focused tone. All business.

"Not sure." Bryan groaned. "Easy."

"Do you want laudanum before I do the sutures?"

"No. Get it over with."

"So you don't know how it happened? Were you at a mine?"

With the water heating, Miriam moved to Alex's side to check for anything she could do to help.

"Someone came and—umph." Bryan grunted as Alex inserted the needle for the first stitch. "...said I was needed at Wilson's Tavern. When I got there, the place was in a brawl." He winced, his hand coming up to his head. "Don't remember anything after that."

Miriam glanced around. Where had the men gone who'd brought Bryan? Surely they knew what happened. But the three of them were alone in the examination room. Alex focused on his sutures, so she hated to bother him. Fitting both crutches under her arms, she swung out to the waiting room. Nobody. She returned to the examination room.

Alex tied off a stitch and leaned back to inspect his work. "That should do it. Now a bandage to keep it clean and salve for the other cuts."

"Should be on the table beside you." Miriam limped to the stove where steam rose from the pot.

His brows gathered as he looked down. "Thanks."

"Alex, did you see where the men went who brought Bryan in?"

"Said they had to go help the others." His attention was focused on his ministrations, so she didn't question him again.

When Alex finally stepped back from his brother, Miriam held a mug of willow bark tea up to Bryan's mouth. "Have a sip."

He obeyed, and she continued to coax him until the cup was empty.

"Would you like more?"

"No. Just sleep." His good eye drifted closed, and his words slurred.

She glanced up at Alex, who stood at the stove cleaning the tools he'd used. He spoke in a quiet tone. "We'll let him rest."

Miriam limped over to join Alex with Bryan's empty mug. "I can clean these." She nudged his arm with her elbow.

"I'll wash, and you dry." His voice had a tired, no-nonsense tone that stopped her from insisting. She picked up a clean drying cloth from the nail on the wall.

Alex didn't speak as they worked, but tension hung heavy around them. She dared a glance when he handed her the dripping washbasin, now clean after he'd almost scrubbed the porcelain finish off it. The muscles in his jaw flexed.

With nothing left to wash, Alex moved the pot of dirty water to the back of the stove and dried his hands on a towel. He turned around and leaned against the oven handle, crossed his arms, and stared at the resting form of his brother.

What was spinning through his mind? Miriam eyed him as she dried the basin and placed it on the work table. His back stood rigid. Every muscle in his body seemed tight enough to snap.

She reached a tentative hand up to cup his shoulder. He made no sign of recognition, except the Adam's apple that bobbed at his throat. Seeing him like this started an ache in her chest. She kept her hand in place, gently sliding her thumb back and forth on the brown cotton of his shirt.

They stood like that for several minutes, watching Bryan as his chest rose and fell in a steady rhythm. Should she say something? But what could she say that would ease Alex's pain? How would she feel if Gideon was carried home beaten and bloody? Of course. The same way she'd felt when she and Leah had found him half-dead in a cave after he'd been mauled by a bear. Scared spitless. Just months after their middle brother, Abel, had been killed by a grizzly, Gideon's attack had broken open too many fresh scars.

Her heart raced in her chest. What could she say now to help Alex? Nothing. But she could be here for him. As long as he needed her.

"I can't lose another sibling."

She almost jumped at the sound of Alex's voice. Raw. Like a knife had scraped his throat, leaving it bloody and aching.

Miriam tightened her grip on his shoulder. "Have you...lost another brother?" Her own loss—the chasm left by Abel's death—gaped wide before her.

"Britt. My sister."

"Oh, Alex." She laid her head against his shoulder. Such a paltry gesture. But she needed to touch him. A physical way to show her grief.

Several moments passed before he spoke again. "It

was my fault."

His fault? Questions raced through her mind, but she didn't move from her spot beside him. Had he been the attending physician? Surely not. Oh, that would be too much for a person to bear.

"She was seven." He swallowed, and his voice grew a little stronger as he continued. "Followed me everywhere I went. Britt was…special. Cute red curls and freckles, and the prettiest blue eyes. People loved her. How could they help it? She could charm a rock into smiling."

He cleared his throat. "Dad sent me out on deliveries one day. But I was miffed, because I really wanted to play ball with Bryan and his friends. Britt, she tagged along." His voice broke, and he paused.

"She had a breathing condition, where sometimes her lungs would only function to partial capacity. I was a stupid lout and jogged the whole way. Never slowed down to let her catch up or rest. By the time we got home, she could only draw tiny breaths. Dad tried every remedy he knew, then sent Bryan for the doctor. Her lungs stopped working before the man could get there."

Oh, Alex.

"Watching her die was the worst. I'd caused it, and yet there was nothing I could do." His voice broke on a sob.

Miriam wanted to hold him. Pull him into her arms and console him. But she stayed in place at his side. She did, however, run her palm down his arm and slip her hand into his.

After a moment, she dared to speak. "You were only a boy, Alex. You didn't know what would happen."

His shoulder tensed, but she forged on. "Her life was in God's hands. He took her to a better place, where she didn't have to struggle to breathe." Her gaze landed on

Bryan. "Your brother's different. Alex, is there anything life threatening about Bryan's condition?"

He stood quiet for a long moment. Had she gone too far? "I won't know for sure if there's internal damage for a day or two."

Her heartbeat quickened. "Do you see signs of it?"

A long sigh. "No."

She squeezed his fingers. "He's in God's hands."

How long did they stand there? Time faded into oblivion. At last, Alex exhaled a long breath.

Miriam straightened, pulling away from his side to examine his face.

"I should probably see if I'm needed at Wilson's." Tight lines gathered under Alex's eyes, a clear hint of the strain that weighed on him.

Her chest ached with the desire to unburden him. "I'll tend Bryan."

At last his gaze found hers. Searching.

She met his look, willing her eyes to show the love and compassion and hope that welled in her chest.

He squeezed her hand. "Thanks."

"What should I give for a stomach ailment?" Miriam leaned around the open door frame to Bryan's quarters. "Mrs. O'Leary's here with her two youngest. Said they've been vomiting all morning."

His brows scrunched where he lay on a low bed in the corner. "Sid and Malcom? I'll come."

"Don't you dare."

Whether it was her command or the pounding in his

head, Bryan sat up only halfway before he stopped. His hand crept up to grip his temple. Between his eye—which was still mostly swollen and glowed a mixture of red, blue and black—and the scrunched expression of pain on his face, the poor man was pitiful.

"Give them each a dose of the blackberry tonic." He sank against the pillow. "Tell her to have them drink peppermint tea and eat dried bread. And keep them away from the girls."

"Thanks." Miriam hobbled on the single crutch back to the front examination room. As she neared the door, the sound of retching filtered into the hallway. She lengthened her stride. Poor thing.

The red curls of the youngest, two-year-old Sidney, bent over a washbasin when she entered the room. His mother cradled him while the little shoulders jerked with each heave. At last he raised his head, chest rising and falling in quick, exaggerated breaths.

Miriam grabbed a cloth from the washstand, dipped it in the water and wrung it out, then handed it to Mrs. O'Leary. The lad's eyes rimmed bright red against the extreme pallor of his skin.

As Miriam dosed the blackberry juice tonic, she talked through Bryan's instructions with the harried mother. "Would you like me to make some peppermint tea for them to drink now?"

Mrs. O'Leary scanned her sons. Five-year-old Malcom lay on the examination table with an arm draped over his eyes, while Sidney snuggled in her arms, a little bit of color now coming into his cheeks. "It'll be easier at home."

Miriam's heart went out to the woman. She had her hands full with the children, especially with her husband working long hours at the mine. "If there's anything I can do to help, come back or send word. Please."

After the pitiful family left, Miriam emptied and rinsed the wash basin, then set to work cleaning the examination room. In small spaces like this room, she could limp from one support to another without her crutch. It took a lot of scrubbing to eradicate the foul smell.

At last, she scanned the room. Everything looked back to rights. Her knee begged for a rest, but she needed to check on Bryan again. Grabbing her crutch, she hobbled down the hallway and tapped gently on the door frame that divided the men's quarters from the clinic.

"Enter."

She stepped into the open doorway. "Just stopped by to see if I can get you anything."

He motioned toward the ladder-back chair beside her. "Sit, and fill me in on today's patients."

Miriam hesitated. She did need to rest her knee, and she supposed she could hear if anyone came in, sitting next to the doorway. Easing onto the chair, she recounted events with the O'Leary family, the poultice she'd put on Mr. Yeltson's burn per Bryan's instructions, and the other assorted cuts and colds she'd treated with Bryan's advice.

"I need to make case notes on everyone." Bryan locked his fingers in his hair, allowing his palm to cover his eyes.

"I've been doing that with each one. You can look at the book and add what I missed." She eyed the lines around his good eye. "Tomorrow."

He let out a sigh. "Can't believe this laid me so low."

"If you give yourself time now to heal, you'll spring back quicker."

He dropped his hand and gave her a dark look. "Yes, doctor."

Miriam made a small effort to bite back her smile, but kept her mouth shut.

Bryan glanced toward the window, where the dirty layer over the glass made it hard to see whether the sun really was setting. "Alex not back yet?"

She rose to her feet with the help of the walking stick. "No. Are you ready for dinner?" She needed to get started so it would be ready when Alex did come in from making Bryan's usual rounds.

"Whenever." His words were groggy.

"See if you can get some sleep before it's ready."

As she limped out of the room, the only response she heard was a "Hmmph" from the general direction of her patient. She allowed a grin. Just like Gideon, stubborn and ornery.

Although in this case, God may have used Bryan's hard head as his salvation.

Chapter Nineteen

*A*lex leaned into the clinic door as he pushed it open. The biting wind made his weary bones ache all the more.

Darkness hovered over the front waiting room, broken only by a dim light flickering from the hallway. His nose picked up the aroma of fried ham, and he followed the scent. At least Miriam would have a warm dinner for him.

A movement caught his attention from the open door at the end of the hallway. The door to his and Bryan's chamber. Miriam appeared, with a crutch under one arm and a stack of plates in her right hand. What was she doing in their private quarters? A surge of anger rose in his chest, larger than the small amount of energy he had left to tamp it down.

She smiled when she saw him. "I have your plate ready. Do you want to eat at the table or shall I bring it to your chamber?"

His insides heated another notch. Bring it to his chamber? What a question. Had she spent all day in there with Bryan? "Just give it to me. I'll eat with my brother."

Hurt flashed over her features before she ducked into the examination room that held the stove.

That look was enough to take the edge off his anger. As he proceeded toward his and Bryan's quarters, the encounter played through his mind again. He shouldn't have snapped at her. Miriam wouldn't do anything improper. Right? It just drove him crazy thinking of her being here with Bryan all day long. Even if it was perfectly innocent, wasn't that how he'd come to fall in...love...with her?

Was he in love? His mind and emotions were too tangled to finish that thought right now. And his bones were so weary.

Bryan lay with his eyes closed when Alex entered their chamber. "Your day go alright?" His lids never flickered as he spoke.

Resentment surged through Alex's chest. "Not as well as yours."

His brother's good eye cracked. "You'd rather lie here with your face and ribs busted up?"

"Looks like you've been well taken care of." Alex tossed his doctoring case in the corner and threw his coat on top of it.

The corners of Bryan's mouth curved, but he didn't answer.

Heat flared through Alex's veins. He was being a cad. But couldn't seem to stop himself. Better to get out of here before he did something he already regretted. Alex stalked toward the door where he'd just entered.

"Alex."

He ignored Bryan's call, and almost ran over Miriam in the hallway.

"Alex?" She caught herself and balanced the plate in

her hand.

He brushed past, locking his focus away from her face. *Get out of here.*

"Here's your food."

Her voice echoed with confusion and hurt. Like a knife twisting his gut. Through the front room, he jerked open the door. The blast of winter air slammed into him, and he stumbled forward, gulping in deep breaths.

For several moments he leaned against the side of the building, inhaling the frigid air. His pulse raced as he stared out at the mountains that rose above the tops of the buildings. Majestic. Incredible. Their awe settled over him like a calming mist. What would it be like to stand near the top of these beautiful peaks and see for miles?

The clinic door creaked open, and Alex's muscles tensed. He kept his gaze on the mountains, but watched from the corner of his eye as Miriam slipped outside and closed the door behind her.

She limped toward him, and leaned against the wall with only a few feet between them. Where was her crutch? Even with the limp, her movements were lithe and graceful. A lady strong and capable. His chest hammered.

Miriam didn't speak for several long moments, but stared out at the mountain tops along with him. His mind wouldn't focus on the peaks. Having her so close, his body craved contact. He needed to apologize. His behavior had been rude and way out of line. Exhaling a long breath, he gathered his nerve to speak.

"There's something about them that draws you in, isn't there?"

Miriam's words caught him off guard. Alex's eyes shot to her face, then followed her gaze to the mountains. A wash of awareness settled over him. They'd been her home for years now. "Do you miss the mountains?"

"A little. I miss the peace. The quiet solitude. The views up there are pretty amazing."

A smile pulled the corners of his mouth. "I was thinking they must be."

"When the pass opens, I can take you up and show you my favorites."

His gaze found her face. It glowed in the soft moonlight, her eyes sparkling a dark green. "I'd like that." He swallowed. "Miriam, I'm sorry I was such a lout in there."

She searched his eyes. "Hard day?"

He scrubbed a hand through his hair. "I don't know how Bryan goes into all those hovels and mines every day. With those conditions, no wonder people are sick." Lowering his arm, he locked his gaze with hers. "But that was no reason to be so rude."

A wrinkle formed in the flawless skin of her forehead. "There's something else, isn't there?"

How was she so perceptive? He let out a breath. "It's just…you and…Bryan." His neck flamed. He was an idiot.

She cocked her head, brows furrowing. "Your brother's injured. I only did what was needed—to help him and the patients that came in."

"I know but…the two of you together…all day." Why was he explaining this? He should clamp a hand over his mouth.

The corners of her lips tipped up. "I have to say, he's not as much fun as you."

A surge of heat sluiced through him. What was she saying?

Before he knew what happened, Miriam slipped under his arm. She wrapped her hands around his waist, and snuggled against his side. Her head rested on his shoulder. His arms closed around her, pulling her tighter. Closer.

"I missed you today." Her breath caressed his neck as her words drifted up to his ear. He tightened his hold on her, breathing in the sweet scent of her hair. How did it always smell so clean and fresh? He pressed a kiss on the top of her head. The memory of her soft lips flickered through his mind. He could still taste her sweetness.

But he couldn't make that mistake again. With monumental effort, he loosened his grip. Running his hands down her arms, he separated her clasp and stepped back. As cold air rushed between them, his body craved her warmth. He almost pulled her tight to him again, but instead, raised her hands to his lips. He was struggling on tenuous ground here.

As his gaze found hers, the same heat reflected there that washed through him. But there was more. Uncertainty? Her eyes held a question.

Lord, please don't let me mess this up. "I should walk you back to the boarding house."

Something flashed in her gaze before she turned away, pulling her hands from his grasp. "Let me get my things."

As Miriam disappeared inside, a cold breeze whipped up, cutting through his wool shirt. Its bite helped drown the ache in his chest.

Miriam tore her gaze from the sun shining through the dingy window. Maybe this was a good day to clean the glass. They'd had a warm spell these last few days, which put her in the mood for spring cleaning. Even if it was the first of December.

As she swept the front waiting room, her eyes drifted back through the window to the mountains in the distance. Snow still covered the peaks, but dark spots of pine trees showed where before there had only been white.

Would Gideon and Leah make it through the pass soon? That thought should bring excitement, right? So why the dread knotting her stomach? It would be wonderful to see Leah again. And Gideon too, of course. To hear all the news from the ranch. Be assured everyone was all right.

But when they came, she would have to go back with them. Leave her work in the clinic. Leave the doctors. Leave Alex. The thought made her throat burn. Miriam swallowed down the lump.

She'd even miss spunky Mrs. Malmgren, whose rusty voice penetrated the wall where Alex examined her in the next room.

"I'm getting along just fine, young man. I only wish I could convince my family of that. A bunch of worriers they are."

Alex's deep tenor was too low for her to understand his response. The door opened though, and he stepped out with Mrs. Malmgren's hand tucked under his elbow.

"They live in Carolina, in a little town called Charlotte. That man my daughter married took her all the way across the country and I've only seen those precious grandbabies once."

"What a shame." Alex's voice held that soothing tone that could calm a raging bear. "How old are your grandchildren?"

"Let's see. Marcus is twenty-five, so Clara Lee must be twenty-one. She has the prettiest red hair and freckles, just like I had when I was her age."

"She sounds lovely." Alex shot Miriam a wink as they shuffled through the front room, and she couldn't help but smile.

Mrs. Malgrem's head shot up, her senses acute. "Is that you, Miss Bryant?"

"Yes, ma'am." Warmth crawled up her neck. "How are you today?"

"Fine and dandy. Just had a nice talk with your young man here." Mrs. Malmgren patted Alex's arm.

"He's, um, not…" Miriam turned away, resuming her sweeping while her face commenced smoking. "I'm glad you're well."

Mrs. Malmgren only chuckled. "I'll see you youngsters later."

Alex closed the door behind her with a chuckle, but Miriam busied herself with the broom.

"She's something else, that old lady. If I have half that much spunk when I'm her age, I'll count my blessings."

"You'll be a trial to everyone around you." Miriam bent to reach the broom under a chair. Then her mind caught hold of what she'd said. She jerked upright. "Not that Mrs. Malmgren is a trial. I just meant your personality with her spunk could be hazardous." That wasn't much better, but she ducked her chin and focused again on sweeping.

Alex's deep chuckle drifted as he strolled down the hallway.

A knock sounded on the outside door. That was unusual. Most people charged right in like they would any other store in town. As Miriam limped to the door, Alex's footsteps grew louder behind her. Her mouth formed a smile. He was still so protective. Always aware and close by when patients were around.

She pulled the door open. And gasped.

"Miriam?"

"Leah!" She threw herself in her sister-in-law's arms, and reveled in the warm embrace. Closing her eyes tight against the sting of tears that threatened, she breathed in Leah's familiar rose scent.

"I can't tell you how good it is to see you." Leah finally pulled back and held Miriam at arm's length. "You don't look like you wrestled a wildcat."

Miriam grinned. "I'm walking now."

"I see that." A twinkle lit Leah's green eyes, and she pulled Miriam into another hug. "I was so worried about you." Leah whispered the words so only Miriam could hear.

Miriam inhaled a steadying breath. *I will not cry.*

"You ladies may not feel it, but it's a mite cold out here."

Miriam pulled back to see Gideon standing there, blowing puffs of steam into his gloved hands. "Well don't stand there, Gideon. Come inside."

With Leah's hand firmly in hers, Miriam turned to lead them into the clinic. She almost ran straight into Alex. "Oh." Her hand came up to catch herself...on his chest.

He grasped her elbow to help her stay upright, a sparkle in his eye. "Looks like we have special company." Slipping to the side in a smooth action, he motioned them in, then reached to clasp hands with Gideon. "Good to see you, Gideon."

"Alex, I'd like you to meet my wife, Leah."

Leah extended a graceful hand, every inch the lady in her emerald cape and kid leather gloves. "A pleasure, Doctor Donaghue. I can't thank you enough for your care and kindness to our dear Miriam." Withdrawing her hand from Alex's, she slipped it through Miriam's arm and pulled her close.

"It was a pleasure, madam." His eyes found Miriam as his mouth turned up. "A true pleasure."

The heat crawling up Miriam's neck would show on her face any minute. Time to change the subject. "Where are you staying?"

"Not sure yet. Had to stop and check on you first."

Miriam eyed her brother. "Mrs. Watson told me yesterday she had an open room upstairs. I doubt she's filled it. I'm staying downstairs."

"Perfect." Leah squeezed Miriam's arm. "You can ride with us in the wagon."

Miriam cut a glance at Alex. "I, um, still have things I need to do here. Why don't you get settled in, then come back for dinner?"

Leah raised a brow. "You have things to do here." She said it as a statement not a question, but the look in Leah's eyes made it clear Miriam would be required to answer when they were alone. "Of course. What say we come get you for dinner at Aunt Pearl's Café around six?"

She raised her gaze to Alex. "Doctor Donaghue, I hope you and your brother can join us. It's the very least we can do to thank you for your excellent care." Her eyes scanned Miriam from top to bottom. "I see our sister is much recovered."

Miriam bit back a grin. How wonderful it was to see her dear friend again. Even if Leah was a bit too perceptive.

Chapter Twenty

Through the afternoon, the knot in Miriam's stomach wound tighter. Gideon and Leah would expect her to go back up the mountain with them. But she wasn't ready. Had more to do here. Working with Alex and Bryan, helping the good people of this town. For once in her life, she was doing something that mattered.

"I put the closed sign up."

Miriam glanced at Alex as she wiped the counters in the examination room.

"Penny for your thoughts?" He strolled to her.

She looked down at the damp cloth in her hand. "Just thinking how much I'll miss this."

He stopped, only a couple of feet between them. What she wouldn't do for him to wrap her in his arms, and tell her to stay.

"When do you leave?" His voice held a hollow tone.

Miriam chanced a look at his face. Those amber eyes didn't hold their normal glow. Didn't share a glimpse into his soul like they normally did. Instead, they were almost shuttered. "I…I'm not sure."

He nodded and turned away, tightening the vise that already constricted Miriam's chest.

Gideon and Leah were right on time, but Bryan still hadn't come in from his rounds when they arrived.

"I'll leave a note for him, and he can join us later." Alex scribbled on a slip of paper before he ushered them through the front door.

Miriam eyed the wagon. "You didn't have to hitch the team for me. I walk back and forth to the boarding house every day."

Leah stepped forward and slipped her hand in Miriam's arm. "Tonight, we'll pretend it's a carriage."

With Aunt Pearl's Café just down the street and around the corner, it wasn't long before Gideon reined the horses in. Alex leaped from the wagon bed and reached up to help Miriam down, while Gideon assisted Leah from the other side. Alex's hands were strong on her waist, lingering for several extra moments as his gaze found hers. Miriam fought the desire to wrap her arms around his neck.

Inhaling a shaky breath, she stepped back. His gaze softened, and he extended his elbow. "Might I escort you, m'lady?"

"Thank you, kind sir." Hopefully, her cheeks wouldn't be as red as they felt.

Aunt Pearl herself greeted them as the group entered the restaurant. "Land sakes, if it ain't the Bryant's. Got a table for ya right by the window."

"Thank you, Aunt Pearl. I've been craving your sweet cinnamon rolls for weeks now." Leah graced the woman with a soft smile as Gideon tucked her into the chair beside Miriam.

"Got a batch in the oven now. I'll bring 'em out while

they're warm." She glanced around. "I'm a bit shy of servers these days. I'll get some coffee for you folks."

As soon as the woman left their table, Miriam turned to her brother and sister-in-law. "Did you have trouble coming down the mountain?"

"Not bad." Gideon's usual succinct answer.

She pestered him with questions though, until he finally brought her up to speed on the ranch and animals.

"John's taking care of things for a few days. I moved the animals to the smaller south pasture so they'd be closer to his place."

Their food came, and conversation lulled for a moment while they dug into the corned beef and cabbage.

Leah was the first to speak. "Miriam, I received a letter from Emily, my friend in Richmond. She's excited we're coming, but won't be able to tour the Northern cities with us. Her sister's bedridden these days, and Emily doesn't feel she can leave for so long."

Despite Leah's calm tone, Miriam could hear the threads of disappointment. "I'm sorry, Leah. That would have made the trip perfect."

Leah's smile was a little too bright. "It'll still be wonderful. I can't wait for you to see the ocean, Miri."

As the conversation continued, Miriam couldn't help but dart glances in Alex's direction. At first he seemed to follow the topic, but after several minutes, he barely raised his gaze from the food on his plate.

Bryan joined them halfway through the meal, bringing an interruption that eased the tension building in Miriam's shoulders. He and Gideon chatted about the latest news around town, including word that the local banker, William Clark, had just invested a chunk of funds in the Dexter 10-stamp mill for processing silver ore.

"I imagine we'll have another boom of miners and fortune hunters come spring." Bryan leaned over his plate. "As long as the mines keep producing the way they've been."

At last, Leah placed her cloth napkin on the table. "Gentlemen, as much as I've enjoyed this, I have some things at the boarding house I'd like to show Miriam. May we bid you good evening?"

Gideon's face fell, and he started to stand, but Leah reached a hand to halt him. "Stay and visit. That'll give Miriam and I time to catch up."

His mouth pulled on one side. "You'll do better without me there."

The men stood with them, and offered polite goodnights. Miriam tried to catch Alex's eye, but he kept his face averted. Something was wrong, but she couldn't quite put a finger on it. Like a barrier had risen between them as the evening progressed.

Leah was silent as they strolled arm in arm to the boarding house next door. Miriam tried to use the opportunity to sort her thoughts, but they were in such a muddle she hadn't made any progress when they stepped through the wooden front door.

"I put a satchel of clothes and things in your room. Mrs. Watson opened it for me." Leah steered Miriam toward her first floor chamber.

"Thank the Lord."

"I can't imagine how you've managed, Miri." Leah held her at arm's length. "This is new, isn't it?"

Miriam pressed a hand against the creamy lace of the shirtwaist Alex had picked out for her. "Isn't it lovely? I only had the one torn dress, so Alex brought this for me."

Leah's face took on an expression Miriam hadn't seen before. Calculating. Suspicious. Intrigued. "Come sit on the bed and tell me about Doctor Alex Donaghue."

What was there to say? That he was the kindest, funniest, most wonderful man she'd ever met? That she'd lost her heart to him, but he didn't seem to feel the same? That even though he'd given her the best first kiss she could have dreamed of, he seemed afraid to get near her now?

No, she definitely wasn't ready to bare her soul about Alex. Not until she could figure out where she stood with the man. Did he like her or not? He gave off too many conflicting signals.

"So…?"

Miriam sat on the bed and snuggled the pillow. "He's a great doctor. Very good with his patients."

"Good with patients like…you?" Leah's voice had a sing-song quality.

"*All* his patients."

"How do you feel about his other qualities?" Had Leah always been this pushy?

Miriam met her gaze squarely. "He's a fine man, and that's all I plan to say on the subject tonight."

Leah threw up her hands with a groan. "You're killing me." Her shoulders slumped and she reached for Miriam's hand. "All right, I'll let you off the hook. Tonight. Don't think I'm blind, though." With brows lowered, she gave Miriam a knowing look. "That boy's smitten. And you're not far behind."

Miriam nibbled her lip. Smitten?

Leah leaped to her feet. "Now, let me show you what I brought."

"I'm so happy for you, Mrs. Garner. A little brother or sister for Henry. I'm sure Mr. Garner is beaming."

Alex sat at the desk as Miriam assisted their patient to the front door. He should be making case notes, but couldn't keep his mind from following their conversation. Miriam had proved an invaluable help with his female patients who were in the family way. She calmed their unease, doted on each woman, and related in a way he never could.

He let out a long breath, but it did nothing to ease the hard knot in the pit of his stomach. Gideon said they'd be leaving tomorrow. Miriam with them.

What was he going to do without her? Elbows on the desk, he dropped his head in his hands and scrubbed his fingers through his hair. *God, what can I do to make her stay?* Nothing. She'd healed amazingly fast. He had no right to ask her to stay on and work at the clinic.

Maybe he could go up and visit her on the mountain. Half a day's ride wasn't so far really. Not like she was going across the country. Yet. He let out another sigh. They were planning a trip back East, and from the sounds of it, she'd be gone six months at the very least. The journey sounded like all Miriam's dreams come true. Traveling in luxury. Seeing famous sights. She deserved every moment of it. The chance to live as an elegant lady of leisure, and attend balls and parties.

His stomach clenched at the thought of her dancing in another man's arms. Some wealthy aristocrat. That's what she deserved. A man far superior to him. She was worth so much more than he could give her. Just a simple doctor in a mining town.

Alex rubbed his eyes. He had to let her go.

Miriam pushed the food around her plate as she listened to Gideon rattle on about the supplies he'd purchased at the mercantile. He had everything loaded in the wagon, strapped down and covered in case they had rain or snow on the way up the mountain. Tomorrow. Why did they want to leave so soon? That was a silly question. Of course, Gideon needed to get back to the ranch.

But *tomorrow*? How could she leave the clinic? The patients? Alex? The brothers would have to go back to eating Alex's burned gruel and rubbery eggs. Who would keep the cobwebs away and sweep after the miners came through with their muddy, soot-covered boots? Heaven knew that hadn't been done very often before she came. And what about the babe growing in Mrs. Garner's abdomen? She'd never get to see the child. And Mrs. Malmgren. At least she could count on the feisty older lady to keep Alex in line. A grin threatened a corner of her mouth, but it wasn't hard to overcome as she thought of leaving them all.

"You going to eat that slice of ham?"

Miriam looked up at Gideon's question, then back down at the chunk of salted pork she'd been pushing around her mashed potatoes. "I guess I'm not that hungry."

"Mind if I take care of it?" Gideon's eyes held a covetous gleam.

She'd barely slid her plate two inches in his direction before his fork swooped in and speared the meat.

"You'd think the man hadn't eaten in weeks." Leah's smile had a hint of apology, before she turned a stern gaze on her husband. "If you're still hungry, dear, I see the gentleman behind you hasn't licked the gravy from his fork yet." But the twinkle in her eye belied her sternness.

Gideon gave a casual shrug, a grin tugging at his lips. "Just didn't want good meat going to waste."

"Can't have that." Leah rolled her eyes toward Miriam. But as Leah looked back at her husband, their eyes locked in that sweet, mushy smile where they seemed to forget about everyone around them.

The sight sent a pain through Miriam's chest, all the way to the core of her. Alex had looked at her like that, right before his face had twisted into a tortured expression.

"We'll leave in the mornin' at first light." Gideon popped a chunk of ham in his mouth.

Leah turned to Miriam. "Will that work for you, Miri?"

No. She swallowed. "I guess."

"Doc Alex said your leg's healin' better than he expected. You just have to keep up with the exercises they gave you."

Miriam could only nod, as she dropped her gaze back to her plate and recommenced spreading potatoes.

Chapter Twenty-One

"Are you going to tell me what's eating you?"

Miriam's shoulders tensed as she turned away from Leah's probing gaze. When they'd returned to the boarding house after the meal, Leah had offered to come help Miriam ready for bed. Maybe it had been a mistake to accept the help.

"Miri." Leah's soft tone compelled her.

Could she tell? Leah would probably understand more than anyone. Miriam spun to face her, straightening her spine. "I don't want to go back to the ranch tomorrow."

Leah sank to the bed and patted the spot beside her. "Come sit."

Miriam obeyed, inhaling a deep breath. She raised her gaze to Leah's, and the gentle love shimmering there eased her nerves a little.

"So if I had to guess, I'd say you're not talking about waiting another day." A hint of humor curved her mouth.

Shaking her head once, Miriam collected her words. "I'd like to stay here and work in the clinic." She dropped her gaze to the spray of blue forget-me-nots on the quilt square in front of her.

Leah sighed. "I guess I'm not surprised. How long were you thinking to stay in town?"

Miriam raised her head. "I haven't really thought that far. It just feels right to be here, you know? Like I'm really helping. I've become acquainted with some of the patients, and I love assisting the doctors. It's like I'm finally doing something worthwhile. Helping to make a difference." How could she explain the powerful need that had grown inside her?

Reaching for her hand, Leah squeezed. "Have you prayed about this?"

The words struck Miriam somewhere in her core. Had she? Not really. Not seeking God's direction. In fact, these last few weeks since she'd been up and moving around, she'd barely stopped to spend her usual morning time with the Lord. *I'm sorry, Father.* She forced herself to meet Leah's gaze. "Not as much as I should have."

"Can we pray now?" Leah's soft voice poured over her like honey soothing a sore throat.

Miriam nodded, then bowed her head.

Leah's words were simple, spoken from a depth of spirit so strong Miriam could almost feel the connection with their Heavenly Father. "Lord, please fill Miriam with wisdom to discern Your will, and show her Your peace as she walks in the plan You have for her. In Christ's name, Amen."

When Miriam opened her eyes, the glimmer in Leah's matched what she felt.

"I always knew God had big plans for you, love. But I prayed they wouldn't take you away from me." Leah pulled her into a tight hug, and Miriam sank into it. Leah was the friend and sister, and sometimes even the mother, she'd always craved.

After a moment, Leah pulled back, holding Miriam's shoulders at arm's length. "This wouldn't have anything to do with a certain young doctor who's smitten, would it?"

Heat surged up Miriam's neck, and she fought the urge to cover her burning ears. "Alex has been very proper."

"Glad to hear it." Leah slid her hands down to grasp Miriam's. "And you can be sure I'll be praying for him, too."

Nibbling her lower lip, Miriam couldn't quite bring her focus up to Leah's face. "Do you think Gideon will be terribly angry?"

"He'll be worried sick." Leah squeezed her hands again. "But you let me talk to him first. He'll be all right. Most likely."

"Will you still leave tomorrow?"

Leah's mouth pressed. "I bet we'll stay one more day. At least I hope so." Her eyes grew soft as they roamed Miriam's face. "We may not be able to come back down the mountain until winter's over."

Relief loosened the muscles in Miriam's neck. At least she had one final day to enjoy them.

Leah rose from the bed, her posture ever erect and graceful. "Now, it seems I have something I need to discuss with your brother." Leaning close, she kissed Miriam's cheek. "Goodnight, love. I'll see you in the morning."

Alex pushed another log into the fire in the cook stove, but even the heat from the blaze inside couldn't burn away his bad mood. Miriam would leave today. Gideon had said as much at dinner two nights ago.

She hadn't come to say goodbye yet, so they must be

getting a late start. Right? His heart beat faster. She wouldn't have left without saying goodbye, would she?

This last month had been too good to be true. Meeting Miriam, having her so eager to help around the clinic. She was an amazing lady. Intelligent. Caring. Fun. But what had he been thinking to imagine there could ever be anything serious between them? Even after she was no longer his patient, their goals were so different. She wanted to travel. Live a life of luxury. And she deserved it, too. Deserved to be treated like a princess. Deserved to be so much more than the wife of a simple doctor in an uncivilized mining town.

With a sigh, Alex rose and turned to look through the window at the mountain peaks on the horizon. It's a good thing he'd worked so hard to keep some semblance of a boundary between them. Except for that kiss. The memory of it flowed through him even now, over a week later. That kiss still tortured him.

The hinge on the front door squeaked, and the sound of a wagon passing outside grew louder. Patients already? Or the Bryant family coming to say farewell? With a tight chest, he strode toward the front room.

He almost bowled Miriam over as he turned the corner, and grabbed both her elbows to keep her upright. "So sorry."

"Oh my." Her cheeks and nose were flushed red from the cold, and she wore a navy wool coat. "Sorry I'm late. How does bacon and biscuits with gravy sound for breakfast?"

His stomach clenched. She was close enough he could smell the rose scent in her hair. And why was she talking about breakfast? He took a step back, releasing her elbows. "You, uh, don't need to worry about cooking today. I'm sure Gideon wants to get an early start."

Her brow pinched, then smoothed as understanding and a suspicious twinkle dawned in her green eyes. "They're going to stay one more day, since I won't be going back to the ranch with them. By the way, would you mind if I take the afternoon off? Leah wants to take me shopping, since I'll need some things for the rest of the winter."

What was she saying? His mind honed in on one fragment. *I won't be going back to the ranch with them.* Did that mean she was staying in town? Here? All winter? His heart soared, but he couldn't let himself believe it yet.

His hands gripped her shoulders. "Are you saying you want to hang around here for the winter?"

Her face took on that shy smile. "If you'll let me."

Joy surged through him. He almost picked her up and swung her in a circle, but caught himself just in time. Instead, he pulled her tight against him, wrapping his arms around her. With her touching him—so close—his pulse sped and his mind recalled that kiss again. Oh, sweet peppermint, but he wanted another. Leaning his head back, he clamped his lips against a groan. This might be the hardest winter of his life.

Miriam raised the soft cotton cloth to examine the tiny checkered pattern.

"That would make a pretty accent material for a spring overskirt." Leah peered over Miriam's shoulder. "Can you imagine it with ruffles trailing down the side and over a low bustle?"

Or imagine how nice it would look as a man's shirt. In her mind's eye, the fabric stretched across Alex's shoulders, tapering to his trim waist. She nibbled her lip. Would it be proper for her to make him a shirt? Probably not. Miriam dropped the cloth back on the stack.

"Do you want to purchase some to make a dress over the winter?" Leah's gaze scanned her face.

"Not right now." Miriam tried to affect a casual air.

Leah slipped a hand around Miriam's waist as they strolled down the aisle away from the cloth and notions. "All right. But you know, Gideon spoke with Mr. Lanyard, and his account is available to you at any time. If you need something, just come get it."

Miriam smiled, leaning into her friend's shoulder. "I really am going to miss you. I hope you'll come to town every chance you get."

"You better believe it." Leah squeezed Miriam's side. "Now tell me, what do you do at the clinic all day?"

"Oh, I keep the place clean, launder dressings, and sterilize supplies. I help clean and bandage wounds, keep the inventory, and sometimes I get to assist with surgeries. Alex is even teaching me how to make some of the medicines from herbs and plants. He said we'll plant an herb garden in the spring, like the one his family has for their apothecary shop in Boston."

"With all you do, no wonder the doctors can't survive without you."

Even though Leah's words hinted at teasing, heat crept up Miriam's neck. How was Alex doing this afternoon? Managing okay by himself? Of course he was. He'd taken care of things alone at the clinic long before she arrived.

Leah stopped to face Miriam. "I'm teasing, Miri. But I see how your face lights up when you talk about your work. I hear the excitement in your voice. You love it, don't you?"

Miriam's chest squeezed. "I do. I'm finally doing

something that feels like it matters." She grabbed Leah's hand and squeezed. "Don't worry about me, Leah. I'm in the right place for now."

In the right place. Miriam's own words echoed through her mind as she sat on her bed in the boarding house. She fingered a corner of the linen-bound Bible in her lap—one of the items Leah brought from the cabin. It'd been so long since she'd sat and talked to God. But why had she stopped? If she was honest, it wasn't because she'd been stranded at the clinic with no Bible. Hadn't Alex brought her their copy along with the other books?

"I'm sorry, Lord." She whispered the words, squeezing her eyes tight. "I'm sorry for neglecting you." The quiet of the room didn't change, but Miriam's spirit seemed a touch lighter. A bit more open.

Lifting her eyes, she flipped the Bible open. Leah's question from the night before still burned in her mind. She hadn't prayed about whether God wanted her to stay in Butte and work at the clinic. Hadn't prayed for His guidance. "Lord, how can I know I'm in the right place? Show me."

Her fingers flipped aimlessly through the first half of the book. Wasn't there a scripture about God having plans for her? Maybe in one of the larger prophet books. It seems like she'd marked it when Leah first showed her the verse. In Jeremiah, her eyes landed on a passage, underscored by a charcoal line.

For I know the thoughts that I think toward you, saith the

Lord, thoughts of peace, and not of evil, to give you an expected end. Thoughts of peace and not evil. What a wonderful image. But how to get that "expected end?"

She thumbed through several pages. There was a verse Leah loved at the beginning of Proverbs. Within seconds, Miriam found the page.

Trust in the Lord with all thine heart; and lean not unto thine own understanding. In all thy ways acknowledge Him, and He shall direct thy paths. The words struck her like a blow to her chest. In *all* thy ways acknowledge Him. She'd always tried to obey Scripture. But only for the easy things. No lying, stealing, or slandering. Mama and Pa had impressed right and wrong on her from her earliest days. But looking to God for direction? Her chest burned from conviction.

"I'm sorry, Lord." She whispered the words. Her fingers searched the words, as though compelled. She landed in Psalms, and her eyes roamed the page, settling on chapter thirty-seven.

Trust in the Lord, and do good; so shalt thou dwell in the land, and verily thou shalt be fed. Delight thyself also in the Lord; and he shall give thee the desires of thine heart. Delight in the Lord. Her soul soared as she read the words. Holding the Bible close, she pressed her eyes shut. "Father, I want to be in Your will. I'm so sorry I haven't sought You the way I should. Please show me where You want me."

An image flashed in her mind. Alex, with that half grin on his face, eyes sparkling. "Lord, even with Alex. Please show me what to do. As much as I love the man, I get so frustrated when he keeps himself distant. Is that You keeping us apart?" She sat still for a moment, her soul troubled. *In all thy ways acknowledge Him, and He shall direct thy paths.* The words from Proverbs. "Father, I give you Alex. Please direct me in Your path."

As she kept her eyes closed, it was like the weight on her shoulders lifted, releasing her spirit to a freedom she hadn't felt in months. Maybe years. She sank against the pillow behind her, savoring the moment. "Thank you."

Chapter Twenty-Two

*M*iriam poured enough water to fill the coffee pot, then slid the carafe to the warmest part of the stove. They went through more coffee than the café at lunchtime. At least it seemed that way.

Picking up the mug she'd filled with the last of the pot's contents, she headed toward the front room where Alex chatted with Mrs. Malmgren. The sassy older woman seemed to especially enjoy his company. Although who wouldn't? Surely the woman got lonely at times. Not only had her husband passed away last year, but now she'd lost the last of her sight. How did she manage? Even with the occasional burns and scrapes that brought her into the clinic, the woman was a marvel. And she never lost her fearless approach to life. Plenty of humor and spunk wrapped in that gray-haired package.

"Here you go." She placed the mug in Mrs. Malmgren's hands, making sure the woman's grip was strong before she released it.

"Bless you, dearie." A smile formed on her lips. "I was just telling your young man I received a letter from my daughter with the most exciting news. My granddaughter's coming to spend a few months with me in the summer. I guess all their worryin' might be worth it to see my Clara Lee again." Her mouth twitched.

Miriam nibbled her lip at the mention of Alex as her "young man." But Mrs. Malmgren's excitement was so strong, better not to douse it by correcting her. "That's wonderful news. I can't wait to meet her."

As she patted the woman's shoulder, a wagon passing outside the window caught Miriam's attention. The stoop of the man's shoulders and the floppy brim of his hat were unmistakable.

She sprinted toward the door as fast as her limp would allow. Throwing it open, she paused to take in the wiry old man reining in his team of mules at the hitching post. "Ol' Mose!"

He pulled up straight at the sight of her, blinked twice, then doffed his hat and slapped it against his leg. "Woowee, if it ain't Miz Miriam. Didn't 'spect to find anythin' prettier here than them homely docs." His eyes twinkled.

A rush of moisture stung her eyes. Ol' Mose had been a dear friend of her family for as far back as she could remember. Probably as long as he and his freight wagon had carried supplies between Fort Benton and Helena.

"Ol' Mose, I'm so happy to see you. Come inside and visit a while." She stepped aside and held the door open. "I put a fresh pot of coffee on, and there's still biscuits and ham left from breakfast."

He climbed down from the wagon, his movements slow and stiff. "Can't say as I'd ever turn down an offer like that, but what're you doin' at the clinic, Miz Miriam. Don't look like yer sick. Figured you an' yourn'd be high up on the mountain with this snowstorm acomin'."

"I'm helping out at the clinic through the winter." Miriam followed him through the door. "Have you met Doc Alex?"

Ol' Mose pulled up so quick, she almost bumped into him. Miriam stepped around to see what caught his attention.

Mrs. Malmgren.

His face formed a lop-sided grin, evident even through his whiskers, and he rolled the brim of his hat with both hands.

"Mrs. Malmgren, may I present a dear friend of mine, Mr. Mose..." She skimmed her memory. What was his last name? They'd called him Ol' Mose as far back as she could remember.

"Moses Calhoun, ma'am. But most folks call me Ol' Mose. Pleasure to meet you."

Moses? Miriam's mouth tipped, especially since his posture had slackened when she said Missus for Mrs. Malmgren's introduction. Miriam addressed her next comment to the woman. "I've so enjoyed getting to know you these last several weeks. It's a pity I didn't get to meet Mr. Malmgren before he passed away last year."

Ol' Mose straightened next to her. Alex had been watching from Mrs. Malmgren's side with a twinkle in his eye, but now a coughing fit seemed to overtake him. Although the shaking of his chest strangely resembled laughter.

"Why don't the two of you sit and visit while Doc Alex and I pour fresh coffee?" Miriam glided to Mrs. Malmgren's side, extracted the coffee mug from her hand, and led the woman to one of the waiting room chairs.

Ol' Mose didn't need to be told twice, but as he sank into the wooden spindle chair across from Mrs. Malmgren, his feet shuffled uneasily. "Have you, uh, been in this area long, ma'am?"

Miriam retreated toward the hallway, grabbing Alex's hand as she passed.

"What are you doing?" he whispered, as they stepped into the main examination room.

Closing the door behind them, she released his hand and clapped hers over her mouth to cover a giggle. "Did you see the look on his face? I never thought I'd see the day Ol' Mose was smitten silly."

Alex's brows drew low. "Better not to interfere. If he's interested in the woman, let him handle it in his own time."

Miriam raised a brow, then sauntered to the cook stove to fill a tray with coffee mugs. "I'm not interfering, just giving them a minute to get to know each other."

When the mugs steamed with dark liquid and she had biscuits laid out on a plate with ham, she couldn't think of any other reasons to dawdle. Alex picked up the tray and followed her from the room.

"You really know Jim Bridger and Jedidiah Smith?" Mrs. Malmgren's voice didn't shake like usual.

"Sure do. Still run into ol' Jim at the Fort ever so often. Most of the ol' trappers have moved on, though. Can't make a livin' at it like we used to."

They looked up as Miriam and Alex approached. "How're you likin' the Territr'y, Doc?"

Alex shot a glance at Miriam as he eased into a chair. "Couldn't ask for a better place to call home."

After several minutes of comfortable conversation, the door opened and a lanky man with a shock of orange hair stepped in. He wore a layer of dark grime on his face and coat, and clutched a rag over his left hand. "Need the doc."

Jumping to his feet, Alex motioned for the man to follow him down the hall. Miriam stood, too, giving an apologetic smile to their guests. "I'll see if I can help. Please stay as long as you'd like."

Ol' Mose rose to his feet. "I'm overdue at the mercantile as it is. Miriam, I'd be obliged if you'd tell the doc I'll set his crates in the corner there."

Darting a glance at Mrs. Malmgren, she turned a smile at her old friend. "Won't you at least join us at Aunt Pearl's for dinner? Mrs. Malmgren, you'll come too, won't you?"

The older woman hesitated. Waiting for Ol' Mose to answer first?

He obliged. "I reckon' I wouldn't miss it. Miss Annie, your compn'y'd be an extra special honor."

Miss Annie? Miriam fought hard to keep the grin off her face. "Perfect. We'll meet you both at the café at six. Ol' Mose, perhaps you'd be kind enough to see Mrs. Malmgren home now?"

Warmth spread through her, as Ol' Mose helped the blind woman to her feet and tucked her gnarled hand under his arm. "I'd be pleased to introduce you to my travelin' companions, ma'am. It's not often Zeke and Zeb get to meet a fine lady like yerself."

A smile spread across Miriam's face as she thought about Ol' Mose and Mrs. Malmgren. She rubbed the wet cloth over the plate's crusty surface under the dishwater. Who would have thought her old friend would find love at his age? Of course, it may be too soon for love, but there were certainly sparks flying between them.

Alex stepped into the room. "I found two new editions of the *British Medical Journal* in one of the crates Ol' Mose brought." His voice was eager, like she'd just offered him warm cinnamon sweet rolls. Hmm… Not a bad idea. She'd need to add cinnamon to the list for the dry goods store.

"Any interesting articles?" She set the last plate on the stack with the others, then ran her open hand through the now-dirty dishwater. Her fingers didn't find any hidden utensils. Good.

"Every one of them." He dropped into a chair and opened the first page.

She nibbled her lip against a smile. Even grown men had a bit of the boy in them. Picking up the pot of used water, she limped toward the back door. The wooden hinge complained as she pushed it open with her hip. Her knee still had trouble holding its share of her weight, so maneuvering the single step took concentration. A couple steps off the path, she dumped the water, shifting her feet back to keep the drops from splashing her skirt. The next garment she made should be an apron.

Straightening, Miriam glanced toward the outhouse they shared with the business on the street behind the clinic.

A motion flashed at the corner of her eye. Miriam turned just as a powerful blow slammed into the side of her head.

"Ooph!" Her hands hit the ground, her world a flash of black and white sparks.

Damp mud pressed her face. Rough hands jerked her up and through the air. Hot breath swarmed her cheek.

A growl snarled in her ear. "Your lover boy's gonna pay."

Another force slammed into the same spot on Miriam's head, jerking her neck to the side.

And then the blackness closed in.

Alex's eyes scanned the opening paragraphs of the "Address in Public Medicine" section of the magazine. Strides were being made in sanitary work. Excellent.

A noise broke his attention, and he raised his head to listen. Silence. No, there it was again. A scuffling sound. "Everything okay?"

Silence.

"Miriam?" Had she fallen?

The soft bump of wood on wood sounded, and the light in the hallway grew dimmer. Alex leapt to his feet. Something wasn't right. She may have gone on to the outhouse, but he needed to make sure she hadn't fallen in the yard.

With his focus on the door leading to the back alley, Alex almost missed the slip of white paper on the hallway floor.

Picking it up, he held the page close in the dim light so he could read the words scrawled in thick charcoal.

Time to pay for what you done to my brother.

His pulse lurched. What did that mean? Who'd leave the note here in the hallway? With a lurch, his senses came alive.

Miriam.

Alex punched open the door and scanned the yard. A figure disappeared around a building at the end of the street, close to the edge of town. The distance made it hard to tell, but the outline looked like a man carrying a large bundle almost as wide as he was tall. A woman?

Sprinting that direction, he focused on the corner where the man disappeared. *God, don't let me be too late.* Alex slowed beside the building where he last saw them. No one in sight now. Where were all the people? At this time in the early afternoon, at least a few townspeople should be milling about the street. The hair on the back of his neck rose.

He stepped forward, scanning the street to his right, then the pine trees behind the buildings across from him. Had the man ducked into a store? Or disappeared into the woods. *God, what do I do?*

The sharp click of a gun cocking grabbed Alex's attention. He spun around...and his blood ran cold.

A man held a revolver against Miriam's lifeless form.

He suspended her by clutching the back of her dress in one hand. Miriam's head lolled to the side, her arms dangling limp. The shiny metal gun barrel disappeared into Miriam's honey curls.

Alex's breath stopped. Was Miriam dead? *God, no!* Every muscle in his body tensed as he examined her chest. Yes. It rose and fell. Maybe.

It took every bit of his control not to lunge forward and grab her. Knock this man aside, and run with her.

He shifted his focus to the man. The enemy. A flash of recognition struck him. Langley? He searched his mind for the man's given name. *Tad Langley.*

The whole picture crashed down on Alex with blinding clarity. Mick Langley's death from the lung fever. Tad, the younger brother, confronting them at the clinic. The note. *Time to pay for what you done to my brother.*

His gaze drifted to Miriam, but he jerked it back to Langley. He couldn't do this if he thought too much about her. "Your business is with me, Tad. Leave the lady out of it."

A slow smirk spread across the man's unshaven face. "You're right. My business is with you. An' I plan to show you just how hard it is ta watch someone you love die—slow an' miserable-like."

That had to mean Miriam was still alive. His chest thumped faster and rivulets of sweat ran down Alex's back. He had to get her away. But how?

Chapter Twenty-Three

L angley's eyes darted around the street, then landed on Alex again. "Here."

Alex barely had time to prepare as the man thrust Miriam at him. He lunged forward to catch her, scrambling so he didn't stumble and knock them both into a heap. He wrapped his arms around her, lifting and cradling her like a child. A steady pulse ticked through the fabric of her dress. He let out a breath.

What had Langley done that she was still unconscious? Dread washed through him, shortening his breath. If only he could measure the pulse in her neck, and raise her eyelids to see if the pupils were dilated. Had Langley used some kind of drug to knock her out? That might be the best scenario to hope for. If he hadn't overdosed her.

"Spin around an' start walkin'."

Alex's thoughts froze as he met the gaze of the man holding the wooden handle of the Colt. Hatred glittered there. Evil.

He turned, moving slow to keep the man from fingering the trigger. What did Langley have planned for them?

"One wrong move, and I'll shoot you first, then her." Something hard and round jammed into Alex's back. "March toward those trees."

With a deep breath, Alex obeyed. Langley kept the gun in his back, and with Miriam unconscious in his arms, it'd be hard to get a jump on the man. He'd find a chance though.

As they crossed the street, Alex kept his head straight forward, but his eyes roamed the boardwalk, the empty road. Where were all the people?

When they reached the woods, Langley motioned toward a footpath to their right. Alex followed the direction without speaking. This must be one of the trails the miners used as a shortcut from the quarries to town. Which mine was he taking them to? Surely any of them would have people around to help.

Langley's gun pressed harder in his back, and Alex lengthened his stride. A couple of times the path split, and their kidnapper directed which fork to take. They traveled up and down small hills, through rocky and sometimes overgrown terrain. Alex's arms ached, but he tightened his hold on Miriam and trudged forward.

After several minutes, she stirred in his arms. A groan crept from her, sending a wash of relief through him. Whatever the man had done to knock her out was wearing off.

Miriam moaned again, louder this time, and her eyes squinted as they cracked open.

"Sshh," he whispered. Whatever Langley intended, she was probably better off without him knowing she'd regained consciousness.

Her eyes opened wider and she clutched his shirt,

fear and confusion flashing across her face.

He tightened his grip and shook his head just enough for her to catch the movement. But he couldn't hold her gaze long. The trail they traveled was not so obvious now, overgrown by branches and small shoots of trees clogging the path. He slowed to step over a fallen trunk. Where were they headed?

At last, they stepped into a clearing. The winter-brown grass rose to his knees, almost hiding the rocks that cluttered the ground. On one side a hill rose up, a mixture of rock and scraggly pine trees covering its surface.

Langley's gun barrel pushed Alex toward the side of the steep slope. His stomach sank as if he'd swallowed one of the stones he stepped around. A mine? As they neared the stone wall, Alex's fear developed into reality. A hole in the rock face yawned before them.

"Get in," the man barked.

Another jab from the metal poking his back ended Alex's hesitation. He had no other choice. Darkness smothered the instant he stepped through the opening. Alex slowed, trying to feel in front of him with his fingers. The last thing Miriam needed was for him to ram her into a stone wall.

"Stop there."

Alex froze, then strained to see anything in the blackness. His eyes were starting to adjust to the dim light that filtered in from the opening behind them.

Langley fumbled with something, a scraping noise accompanying his efforts. Then a flash of light as a match flamed to life. It illuminated a dirty lantern, which the man lit, then tossed the match to the floor.

"Move on."

The hard metal jammed into Alex's back again, and

he stumbled forward. Regaining his balance, he took a tentative step. The lantern light only illuminated a few inches in front of him, and the wood timbers that lined the shaft quickly closed in as the walkway narrowed. He lost track of how long he walked. With Miriam cradled in his arms, he traipsed blindly through the underground passage. He had to shift almost sideways as the tunnel contracted, so he didn't bump Miriam's head and feet against the wooden braces.

Openings split off to the side in both directions. At one of these, Langley motioned for him to take a path to the right. "Turn here."

Dread settled into Alex's chest as he obeyed. How much deeper would they go?

After several more minutes, his foot struck something solid, knocking Alex off balance. He fell to his knees with a cry, gripping Miriam tight and twisting his body so she didn't bear the brunt of their fall. She screamed, clutching his shirt.

Pain coursed through him, as his knees hit hard stone and something sharp pressed into his left shin. Alex knelt there, sucking in air. His arms rested on the stone floor, still cradling Miriam. "Are you okay?"

"Yes." The word came out in a whisper, but he could hear the fear in her voice.

Alex withdrew one hand and felt for the item poking into his left leg.

Langley shuffled closer, bringing the circle of light with him. Alex craned his neck to see what lay under his limb. A wooden timber. That must have been what tripped him, too. More timbers lay to his left against the wall. His eyes followed the edge of light up and around. The shaft was bigger here. Wider, and maybe taller.

"Get her over by the wall." Langley motioned toward an empty spot beside the stack of wood.

Alex's gaze came back to Miriam. She stared up at him with wide, fear-filled eyes. Protection surged through him. He tried to give her a reassuring smile, but his tight lips wouldn't obey. He had to find a way out of this mess. Once he had Miriam settled, maybe he could overpower their captor.

Alex's arms ached as he helped Miriam stand on shaky legs. He kept both hands around her as she shuffled over to the spot Langley pointed out.

"Make her sit."

Why did he still speak to Alex, since Miriam was awake? Trying to keep a mental distance from her? Maybe the man thought that would make it easier to kill her when the time came. If that was the case, maybe they could use that weakness against him. As much as Alex wanted to protect Miriam from having to interact with the man, maybe forcing the issue would weaken Langley's defenses.

Thoughts whirled through Alex's mind as he helped Miriam settle on the stone floor. "Are you all right?" he whispered again, catching her gaze.

"Shut up!" Langley roared.

Alex clamped his mouth shut, but studied Miriam for an unspoken response. She nibbled her lip and nodded once, but Alex could see pain clouding her eyes. Desire to help her coursed through every part of him. As he studied her eyes, one pupil looked larger than the other. A trick of the light? Or was it a head injury that had kept her unconscious?

Alex spun toward their captor, clenching his fists. The urge in his blood toward this man had nothing to do with healing.

"Get that rope." Langley stood about six feet away

with both feet planted, pistol pointed straight at Alex's chest.

Alex didn't move. Locking eyes with the man, he forced himself to breathe, drawing in dank air. Could he lunge forward and tackle Langley before he got off a shot?

"The first bullet goes in yer heart, Doc. The second one in hers." Langley's voice dropped in the silence like boulders in a creek, sinking into Alex and leaving a metallic taste in his mouth.

After one more moment, he turned in the direction Langley had pointed. A coil of rope he hadn't seen before was tucked next to the stack of timbers.

"Take a piece an' tie her hands tight."

Bile rose up in Alex's chest as he knelt beside Miriam with the braided leather rope.

Her eyes shimmered with...forgiveness, courage? A whole host of emotions he couldn't stop to examine. She held up her wrists, palms facing.

"Behind her." Langley growled the words.

Miriam scooted around and crossed her wrists behind her. They were so delicate and creamy, even in the dim light of this tunnel. Except for the outline of red mottled skin on her right wrist where new flesh grew to replace burned skin. Alex couldn't bring himself to wrap the cord tight. But if he left it too loose, Langley would likely jerk the knots much tighter. He tied them as loose as he dared, then slipped his hand into Miriam's and gave it a quick squeeze.

"Now her feet."

Alex cringed at the gruff command, and his stomach churned at the thought of what he was being forced to do. Would Langley tie him next? Alex had to get control of that gun. Maybe he could use one of the wood timbers as a weapon. A quick glance dashed his hopes. They were as tall as he was, and looked much too heavy for him to move quickly. Maybe the lantern then? He could swing it like a club. If he could get Langley to set it down.

"Hurry up."

Alex tightened his jaw as he nudged Miriam's skirt up enough to reveal her leather boots. He took as long as possible with the knots, and Langley scuffed the rock floor as he finished.

When Alex looked up at his captor, the man waved toward an open area beside Miriam. "Lay on yer belly. Hands behind ya."

This was it. Alex would be at a severe disadvantage with his hands and feet bound. Couldn't let that happen. So maybe he'd have the chance to tackle the man when Langley came close to tie him. Alex laid on the floor as instructed and crossed his wrists behind him.

With his head facing the man, he watched Langley set down the lantern and approach. The burly oaf eyed him, holding the Colt well in front and aimed directly at Alex. Did it shake a little? Maybe that was the dance of the flame through the lantern's glass. Langley gripped a piece of rope and tucked the pistol between his knees as he bent over Alex. His grip was like a vice as he seized Alex's wrists and jerked them up to wrap the braided cord.

Alex twisted to the side in a quick motion, drawing his legs forward and kicking hard at Langley's knees.

But the man was too fast. He grabbed the handgun and leaped back in a lightning-fast movement. A mighty boom rent the air. An explosion of sound ricocheting off the stone walls and vibrating the ground beneath them.

Miriam screamed before she could stop herself. Her hands strained at the rope in an instinctive ache to cover her ears. Was that a nitroglycerin explosion? Would the mine cave in around them? She craned her neck to watch for falling timbers. Clouds of dust wafted through the air, but no part of the tunnel seemed to be moving.

"Next time I'll aim fer her."

She jerked her attention back to the man pointing the pistol exactly where he'd said. At her chest. That same area seized. *God, I'm not ready to die.*

"I'll be still." Alex's voice was hard as the stone around them.

Langley slowly lowered the Colt, his gaze flicking between the two of them. He muttered several words Miriam had only heard once, when a group of rough miners came into Aunt Pearl's Café. They'd made her feel dirty then, but now they sank through her veins like ice.

Langley made quick work of binding Alex's hands and feet, jerking hard on the knots with a grunt each time. Miriam's eyes scanned the cavern where they sat. Wooden beams supported the sides and ceiling every few feet. What did Langley intend to do with them? Leave them here to die of starvation? That might be the best possible scenario. It'd give them time to find a way out, even if they had to dig through to the surface.

Langley pulled one final time on the rope at Alex's feet, then backed away. "Get over by that wa—" A fit of coughing interrupted his words. The wet hacking struck a familiar cord in Miriam's mind. Wasn't that the same sound his brother had made before he died? Was this man suffering from the same illness? Another feeling seized her chest. It couldn't be sympathy. Not when the man held a gun on them. But his pistol shook with his shoulders now, as

Langley tried to stop the coughs.

Out of the corner of her eye, she saw Alex slide his legs underneath him. Langley saw it too, because the click of his gun cocking echoed through the tunnel.

Alex froze.

Langley finally stopped coughing, his breath wheezing as he struggled to catch it. "Get over to that wall." He motioned with the gun toward a spot on the wall where Alex would be separated from her by a pile of timbers.

A wave of disappointment washed through her. If she and Alex could sit together, maybe they could try to untie each other's bonds. Or at the very least, she'd have his presence. And maybe they could brainstorm an escape plan together.

Their captor stepped toward the opposite wall, and picked up something just outside the circle of light. A can of some sort. He tucked the pistol in the waistband of his pants, then removed the lid and strode toward her. He veered at the last moment, and dumped the contents over a pile of wood a few feet to her left.

As a sickeningly sweet odor permeated the air, it awakened a terrifying realization.

Langley was planning to set the place on fire.

Chapter Twenty-Four

*T*error roiled in Miriam's stomach. For the first time, it was a very real possibility they might not come out of this alive.

Langley pointed to the spot he'd just doused and glared at Miriam. "Sit there."

She hesitated only a moment. Clenching her lip in her teeth, she scooted up and crawled over the wood planks to where he pointed.

The man turned and retrieved another can, then dumped the contents onto the pile of timbers between her and Alex. He jerked his head toward it, barely glancing at Alex. "You. There."

Alex obeyed, scooting up to sit on the pile of wood. Once he was settled, he looked back at Langley as the man turned away from them. "Your brother was a good man, Tad." Alex's voice rose steady and calming. That reassuring accent he used with patients. No hint of fear. How did he do it?

Langley stopped mid-stride and glared at Alex, then spit onto the floor and tossed the empty can into the darkness. The clatter resounded against the stone walls for several seconds.

"Until you killed him." The venom in his words could have slain a grizzly bear.

"I did everything I could for Mick, but the lung fever was too advanced. I know you miss him, Tad. But killing us won't bring him back."

The man turned with a roar, fists clenched at his sides. For a second, it looked like he might charge Alex and tear him apart with his bare hands. "You killed my brother." Langley stood there, shoulders heaving.

Miriam cringed, willing Alex not to respond. The man was obviously not in any condition to reason with.

After a few moments, Langley spun and stepped back to the far wall where he'd retrieved the cans of kerosene. He knelt down and seemed to be fiddling with something.

The smell of the oil so near made her stomach churn, and Miriam tried not to breathe through her nose. She glanced at Alex, but he stared at their captor, jaw set and mouth pinched in a narrow line.

She sank back against the stone behind her. Was she ready to die? So many things she still wanted to do and see. And she'd never had the chance to tell Alex how much he meant to her. Even if he didn't return the feelings, she loved him with every ounce of her being. That was clear now. Another glance at him sent a surge of longing through her chest.

She turned away and stared down at her skirt. Faces paraded through her mind. Mrs. Malmgren, with her spunky outlook on life. Dirty faces of miners who'd been kind and respectful, many of them with lung illness or breathing difficulty. There were so many still to help. Together, maybe she and Alex could have made a difference.

God, I prayed for Your will. If this is it, be with those

others. Send someone else to help them.

Alex stared at Tad Langley's back as thoughts tumbled through his mind. His own death wouldn't be any great tragedy. Maybe he deserved it after all the times he'd failed with his patients. With Britt.

But Miriam? She didn't deserve to die. Someone so amazing, full of life and kindness, and so many talents. She deserved to marry a wealthy gentleman. Travel the world. Have babies to love.

He swallowed past a hard lump in his throat. He wanted them to be his babies. *God, why are you letting it end like this?* He'd never had the chance to tell her how much she meant to him. To tell her how much he loved her with every fiber of his being. Even though he didn't deserve anyone half as wonderful as her. Still, the unspoken words made his throat ache.

He glanced at Miriam. She stared down at her skirt, mouth pinched in a thin line. She was so brave. Even in the face of death, she wasn't crying. No whimpering or pleading with the man. Just courageous acceptance. Another wave of helplessness washed through him. *God, if there's anything You can do to save her. Please. Help.*

Langley turned from his pile of materials with another can of kerosene. He doused a third stack of wood just outside the circle of the lantern's light. After leaning over his supplies again, Langley straightened with something small clutched in his right hand.

He picked up the lantern from the middle of the floor, holding it close to his face. The light threw an eerie yellow over his skin as he stared into it. Shadows danced across his features, giving him a distorted look. How had Langley's mind become so twisted that he thought killing them would make up for his brother's death? Was it only vengeance he sought?

Still staring into the light, the man chuckled a mirthless laugh. It turned into a cough, though, and he turned to the side as the spasms overtook him. Realization washed over Alex with unmistakable clarity. Tad Langley had the same wet, hacking cough his brother had suffered from. Was he dying of the same lung disease?

The man finally straightened, struggling to catch his breath. His glazed eyes locked with Alex's. "I'll not die...the way...my brother did." His heaving breaths slowed his words, but the message was clear. Langley planned to perish in this tunnel with them.

A cold dread washed through Alex. *Lord, we need Your help here.*

Langley raised the light again, gazing into it. The flame reflected in his glazed eyes.

With a mighty roar, like an Indian war cry, Langley heaved the lantern toward Miriam. It crashed against the wood, splintering into glass pieces. The flame lit the kerosene with a *whoosh!*

Miriam's scream split the air as fire exploded around her.

Alex was on his feet in an instant. A boom exploded through the cavern, and a rush of air whizzed by Alex, striking his upper arm. Pain flashed through the place it touched. A bullet?

"Sit down!" Langley thundered.

Alex fell back onto the pile of wood, gritting his teeth as the pain now came alive, searing his arm. In the corner of his eye, Langley moved toward Alex, a flame in his hand.

With a rush, fire burst around Alex. He fought against it, scooting back to the wall as the flames took hold of his trouser legs.

A scream permeated his awareness. *Miriam.* His mind clearing, Alex rolled over, passing through the flames. Searing heat and fire lit his legs. When he was off the wood, he kept rolling. In seconds, the flame doused.

As he leaped to his feet, the bond at Alex's feet broke free. The fire must have weakened it. With his hands still tied, he sprinted toward Miriam. She'd moved off her pile of burning timbers, too, but now lay in another blaze, as flame billowed from her skirts. She cried out, a sort of half-scream, half-moan.

Alex fought to pull his hands free, but the rope held fast at his wrists. "Roll over!" he yelled. Was it loud enough to penetrate Miriam's pain and fear? With his boot, he pushed against her legs.

She got the idea, and rolled several times until the flame finally burned out.

With that disaster abated, Alex spun to face the next threat. Where was Langley? Flames from the two piles of wood rose almost as tall as Alex, popping and roaring as they devoured the kerosene and wood. And the air.

He spotted Langley, on his knees, doubled over as his shoulders shook in a coughing fit.

Now was his chance.

Eyeing the nearest fire, Alex strode toward it. He turned his back to the fire, and craned to see as he shuffled backward until the cord at his wrists touched the flame. Heat seared his skin, but Alex clamped his jaw against the pain. The moment the rope pulled free, he jerked his arms away and stumbled forward, grabbing his wrists with both hands. The pain almost blinded him as he clutched his burning flesh.

But he still had a job to do. *God, help me.*

Eyeing Langley, he spotted the pistol in the man's front waistband. Alex crept around behind him. He'd have to be quick enough to get the gun before Langley did, but that would be a challenge because of the way the man doubled over from coughing.

Inhaling a breath, Alex lunged, wrapping his arms around the man's thick mass as he reached for the Colt. The force of his charge propelled them both to the ground. Langley cried out, then his body went limp under Alex.

Alex scrambled to turn the man over until a glint of silver appeared within the folds of his shirt. He closed his fists around the wooden handle and jerked it free, then clambered backward until he was a safe distance away. He pointed the handgun at Langley, clutching it with both hands to keep from shaking.

But Langley still didn't move. No coughing. No struggling to rise. Just lay there with his body contorted into the position Alex had rolled him.

Goose bumps raised over Alex's arms, despite the heat from the fire just feet away. Were they safe? Or was Langley bluffing, trying to lull him into a sense of security so he could pounce?

Or had he hurt the man? Nausea rose into Alex's throat. He'd never intentionally caused injury to another human being. It warred against everything within him. Against the Hippocratic Oath he'd sworn to uphold.

Pressure on Alex's arm jerked his attention and he whirled to face the threat.

Miriam.

Pain and fear washed in her eyes through the smoky

haze. He had to get her out of here. He reached for her hand, but stopped. Her wrists were still tied behind her back. Were her feet bound, too?

Alex scanned the area. What could he use to cut the straps? The flames had grown taller beside them, shoulder height now. Any moment they would spread to the timbers that lined the walls and ceiling. They had to get out.

His gaze landed on Langley. The man probably had a knife. And he lay only a couple feet from the flames. Alex crouched by his side, rolling the man toward him as he checked pockets. Nothing. He jerked up the hem of his pants legs. Aha.

Alex yanked the knife free by its bone handle and spun toward Miriam. "Here."

She turned her wrists to him, and he sliced the cord with two tugs of the knife.

"Oohh." He barely heard Miriam's groan over the roar of the fire.

He dropped to his knees and pushed what was left of her burned skirts aside with his arm. The heavy stench of soot clogged his nose, but he forced himself to breathe through his mouth. The first smoky breath almost gagged him, clenching his chest in a cough.

The brown leather of Miriam's boots had turned black. *Lord, please don't let her be burned.* The leather strap binding her legs together split on the first slice of the knife. As his elbow jerked with the effort, it raised the hem of her dress high enough to see red flesh where her stockings had been burned away. His stomach clenched. How much pain was she in? He had to get her back to the clinic where he could tend her wounds.

The sound of coughing brought Alex to his feet. After clearing her lungs, Miriam raised her head to meet his gaze.

Her eyes rimmed red.

Slipping his hand into hers, Alex gave it a quick squeeze. "Let's go." His words came out in a croak. His throat burned.

Alex scanned the cavern. They needed a light to make their way out of the mine. He bent low and pulled a piece of wood from one of the burning piles. Most of it had burned — was still burning — leaving a two foot handle on one end. "Stay close."

He started toward the shaft they'd come through, but stopped when he almost tripped over Tad Langley. The man groaned and rolled onto his back. *What should they do with him?*

Alex glanced at the fire, less than a foot away from the unconscious man's boot. They couldn't leave him here. The man would die in this fiery cave. Alex stared into the pale face on the ground. He tried to summon the anger that coursed through him when he saw Langley holding up Miriam's limp form. But all he saw in his mind's eye was the grief on the man's face when he broke down at the clinic after his brother's death.

How could Alex leave him here to die? A fellow human being? He turned to Miriam. Saw the understanding in her gaze. He thrust the torch into Miriam's hands. "I'm going to try to carry him."

Langley was even heavier than he looked. Alex bent low and tried to hoist him over his shoulder. The first time, they both ended in a heap. Miriam set the flame down and helped lift the man, then steadied them both as Alex crouched under the weight.

"Let's go."

Chapter Twenty-Five

*A*lex stumbled as fast as he could go, doubled over under Langley's weight. Miriam scampered ahead to light the way. Every ounce of his body begged to rest, but Alex pushed on.

They reached the end of the shaft, and Miriam hesitated. Alex dropped to his knees, settling Langley in a heap on the floor. His chest seized from the exertion and from breathing deep gulps of the smoke hanging in the air. It had followed them, drifting down the passageway and filtering through the air they breathed.

"Which way?" Miriam spoke in a loud whisper, the darkness around them cloaking everything in an eerie quiet. The torch she held glowed only red embers now, and it didn't do much more than reveal the outline of her face.

"Go left."

"Wha..." Langley groaned in Alex's arms, but it turned into a fit of coughing. The man's chest shook as Alex kept him draped over his shoulder.

When the coughing finally ended, Alex gave the man a little shake. "Are you awake, 'I'ad?" If Langley could walk out on his own accord, they'd be in a much better spot.

Alex's muscles had no power left. His arms screamed as he gripped Langley's body. He wasn't sure if he could carry himself, much less this giant of a man.

Langley grumbled something incomprehensible, which ended in another phlegmy cough that wracked his body.

When Langley stopped hacking, Alex pushed the man away. "Can you stand up?"

Langley propped his head in a big, grimy paw and groaned.

"We've got to walk out of this mine and get you help, Tad. Stand up now." Alex wrapped the man's free hand over his shoulder and slipped an arm around Langley's bulk. Miriam's glowing stick moved closer, and she positioned herself at Langley's other side.

"One, two, three...up." With a groan and several grunts, they all three stumbled to their feet. "Now walk." Alex mumbled the words as he took an unsteady step.

Langley responded with another fit of coughing. Alex's chest tightened. They had to get the man out. He needed a good dose of fresh air, and medicine to open his lungs.

For a split second, an image of Britt flashed through his mind. Lying in bed while the cough wracked her frail body until her lungs gave out. Alex clamped his jaw against the image. That wouldn't happen again with this man if it took every last ounce of his strength.

The going was slow, especially when the tunnel narrowed and they had to turn sideways. Langley seemed to be coming awake, and bore some of his weight. He kept up a steady stream of coughing though. Had he ingested too much smoke?

After what seemed like days, a faint lightening

appeared in the darkness ahead. Daylight? A flutter of relief sank through Alex's weary limbs.

The light grew, opening into a circle of brown grass and blue sky. If he'd enough strength, he would've cried out for joy.

The moment they stepped onto soft ground, Miriam stumbled and went down. Like a row of dominos, Langley fell next, then Alex. After dropping to his knees, Alex rolled to the side, out from under the weight of the brute they'd just worked so hard to save.

Langley started another coughing fit. He lay face down in the grass, his shoulders jerking with each spasm. The spit that gurgled from the man's mouth dripped black and viscous. Each wracking cough sounded like the last contraction of the man's lungs before they collapsed.

When the coughing spell finally ended, Langley crumbled to the ground, his back rising with each gasp for air. Alex struggled to his knees and leaned close, pressing his ear against the man's back. A gurgling sound accompanied each breath.

Helplessness washed through Alex like water through a pipe. He had to do something before Langley's heart shut down or his lungs caved in. He scanned the area around them. What were the chances he would find an elecampane plant? Possibly a wild cherry tree, but that would take too long to powder the bark, and he had no tools to make an extract.

God, help me help this man.

"What's wrong, Alex?"

His head jerked to meet Miriam's troubled gaze. "I don't have anything to help him."

"If you stay here and pray, I'll run back to the clinic and get what you need."

A surge of anger sluiced through him. "The man's about to die, Miriam. I've seen this before and he won't last until you get back."

She leaned forward to rest her hand on Alex's arm. "Then pray, Alex. Put him in God's hands."

"That won't—" He cut himself off before he spoke the blasphemous words. But bitterness quickly overshadowed the anger in his chest. Britt's lifeless form filled his mind. Pale. Just a ghost of the vibrant child she'd been before he failed her.

"That won't what?" Miriam's voice was soft, yet probing.

Alex sank onto his heels, his chin dropping as he stared at the man's heaving back. "That didn't make a difference with Britt." He mumbled the words, but her quick intake of breath told him she'd understood perfectly.

Another fit of coughing from Langley interrupted their silence. This one was shorter, but the convulsions more severe, if that were possible. They were going to lose him, and there was nothing Alex could do except sit there and watch.

"It wasn't your fault, Alex."

His hands gripped into fists where they rested on his thighs. She didn't understand.

"You were a thirteen-year-old boy."

He clenched his jaw. Nothing she said would change the way he'd failed his sister. If only he could go back in time. Erase that awful day. Or at least take her place on that deathbed.

"Do you think you're powerful enough to change God's will?"

He jerked his head up. "What?"

"God has a plan for every person He creates. He

called you to be His special instrument of healing. But if He has a better plan for the people you treat, nothing you do can change that." Her voice had an edge now. A conviction.

The thought struck him like a blow to the chest. "But..." Was he getting in God's way? "How can he want these people to die? How could he want Britt...to die?" His voice cracked on the last two words.

"Maybe Britt had accomplished what He created her for." The gentleness crept back into Miriam's voice. "And now she's dancing and singing with him in Heaven. No more pain."

The image took his breath away. That's what he'd wanted for Britt here on earth. Had she been enjoying it in heaven all these years? A blanket of peace settled over him, lightening his shoulders.

"Do what God called you to do, Alex. And let Him handle the rest."

Alex's eyes drifted shut as he absorbed the words. *Let Him handle the rest.* He inhaled a deep breath and released it. *God, how could I have it wrong all these years? I want to be Your tool. Use me to help these people, but don't let me forget You're in control.*

Langley started coughing again. Deep, shaking spasms of his whole body.

Lord, I give you care of this man. Into Your hands I commit him. Alex bowed his head.

Help him. The voice was so clear, Alex's eyes flew open to see who had spoken. Miriam leaned low over Langley, brushing the hair from his face and speaking soothing words. Hadn't she heard the voice?

Help him.

Lord? Alex raised his eyes to the clear blue sky. A single white cloud surrounded by a blue so rich no artist could duplicate it. *Is that You, God? Show me how.*

"What's this?"

Miriam's words brought his focus down. She held up a small glass bottle. "It was in his shirt pocket."

Alex sucked in a breath, reaching for the jar with clumsy fingers. Could it be? The white label held words scribbled in his own hand. "Elecampane Root Extract." *Thank you, God.*

His face stretched into a wide smile as he gazed at Miriam. "It's what he needs. Help me turn him so he can sit up."

Langley was barely conscious as they adjusted his position. Miriam propped herself behind his back, since the man didn't seem to have the strength to hold himself upright.

With trembling fingers, Alex poured a hefty dose into Langley's mouth. "That should help right away." He held the bottle up to peer through the amber glass. "There's enough here for one more dose. Just enough until we get him back to the clinic."

He took in Miriam with his gaze. "Do you know how to get back to town from here?"

She looked around, and his eyes followed her stare. There seemed to be an overgrown driveway through the wood to their left. "I should be able to follow that to a road I recognize."

Together they laid Langley down on the grass. The man's eyes cracked open, settling their unfocused gaze on Alex.

"Feeling any better?"

The slightest of nods.

"I'll give you another dose in a few minutes." Alex's mouth quirked on one side. "If I'd known you had elecampane in your pocket, we could have saved us all some worry."

One corner of the man's mouth raised a fraction of an inch as his eyelids drifted shut again. It's a good thing Langley didn't try to talk. His vocal chords would likely take days to recover from the smoke damage.

Miriam started to rise, and Alex scrambled to do the same. As he stepped around Langley's feet, his gaze wandered to the overgrown trail that he hoped led to a road. How far outside of town were they? It had seemed like forever on the walk out here, but they'd probably traveled about fifteen minutes. Still, that was the shortcut. What if she met up with some rowdies on the road? What was he thinking sending a woman—this woman—off by herself in the middle of nowhere?

"I'll be all right, Alex." Miriam slipped her hand into his, pulling his attention to her face.

She was beautiful. Everything about her touched his heart and soul in a way he hadn't thought possible. She cared about people more than anyone he'd ever known. Even this rough miner who'd knocked her unconscious, bound her hands and feet, and tried to burn her alive. Yet, she still ministered to him with compassion and kindness.

He raised his free hand to cup her face, losing himself in her sea green gaze. "You're an amazing lady, Miriam Bryant. How could I help but love you."

Her lips parted as she inhaled a breath.

He was too far gone to turn back now. "You deserve so much better, but I can't imagine my life without you. Please say you'll marry me."

A sheen of moisture washed her eyes, and they glittered in the sunlight. Her mouth pressed tight, as if she were holding back tears. Had he upset her? What was he thinking to propose out here, after they'd just been kidnapped and almost murdered?

He swallowed. "I'm sorry, I shouldn't have sprung that on you. It's just, after today… We never know what tomorrow will bring. And no matter what, I want you with me." He took both of her hands in his own and raised them to press a kiss on her fingertips. "If you want to go back East, we can. We'll tour the world if that will make you happy. Just say the words."

Miriam fought back a sob of joy. Alex loved her. And wanted to marry her. Oh, *God, thank you!* It was too good to be true. She had to get control of her emotions before Alex kept talking and had them on a ship bound for the West Indies.

She pulled her fingers free from his grasp and touched them to his lips. He froze, mid-sentence, and she rewarded him with a smile. "I would love to marry you, Alex."

He closed his hand over hers and planted a kiss on her fingertips, then another on the fleshy part of her palm that sent shivers through her. His brown eyes darkened as he slipped a hand behind her neck and drew her close. His lips settled over hers in a touch gentle and achingly sweet.

Oh, heaven. His kiss was everything she'd dreamed of and so much more. Her whole body answered, filling her response with all the love that had grown within her for this man.

With a groan he tore himself away. His chest heaved as he lowered his forehead to hers. "Have I told you lately how amazing you are?"

Miriam smiled as she worked to steady her own breathing. She cupped his face with her hands, skimming the hint of stubble that had grown since the morning. "You're pretty incredible yourself."

He nipped at her little finger, holding it for a second between his lips. The act made her want to pull his mouth down to hers again.

A cough from Langley broke through her thoughts.

Miriam nibbled her lip. "I'd better go for help."

He blinked, his brows furrowing as if he were trying to interpret her words. Then he planted a final kiss on her palm and stepped back. "I'll go. No telling who you might run into on the road."

A flare of determination whipped through Miriam. "You need to stay with Mr. Langley. I'll hurry, and I'll be *fine*."

As if to prove Alex's necessity, the man on the ground released another deep cough.

Alex glanced between her and Langley, obviously torn.

She squeezed his hand and stepped away. "I'll be back as quick as I can."

"Wait."

Miriam stopped as he closed the distance between them, gripped her shoulders with both hands, then swooped down for another kiss. This was not the gentle caress from minutes before. It spoke of his urgency. His desperation. His desire to control, even though he knew it was beyond his control. It lasted only seconds before he stepped back and released her. "Please be careful."

Her mind still whirled from that kiss, but Miriam gave him a wobbly smile. "God will be with me."

His shoulders sagged. "I know."

Then she turned, gathered her skirts in her hands, and ran.

Chapter Twenty-Six

*T*he overgrown wagon trail did lead to a road. Was it the Mullan Road that led to town? Miriam turned the direction Butte should be. *God, please let this be the way.* She started off in a jog, but the smoke still clouding her lungs made it hard to breathe. Coughing forced her down to a walk, as she doubled over, her chest trying to rid itself of the foreign toxin. When the spasms finally ceased, she raised her head.

The sound of a wagon drifted from around a curve in the road. Glimpses of it flashed through the trees. The murmur of a male voice drifted on the breeze. Singing? Or arguing? A rustle of apprehension ran through her. Maybe she should have let Alex come. She was capable of giving Langley medicine wasn't she? But if something went wrong or the man grew much worse, Alex would know what to do.

Miriam squared her shoulders. And she was more than capable of handling herself on the road. She'd grown up in these mountains, and could always duck into the woods if the man approaching looked unsavory. She strode forward to meet the stranger head on.

"...sweet Betsey from Pike, who crossed the wide

prairies with her husband Ike."

That voice. So familiar. As the wagon passed around the bend, a pair of chestnut mules came into view. And then…

"Ol' Mose!" Miriam broke into a run as her heart soared.

"Well lookee who it is. Miz Miriam. Yer the last person I 'spected to meet up with out here." Her old friend reined in the animals as she reached the wagon side and clutched it, struggling to catch her breath.

"Need your…help."

"Sure thing, missy. What's got you worked up?"

"Alex…there's a man…we were kidnapped." Why couldn't she catch her breath?

"Slow down there."

She spun and waved for him to follow. "Come with me. We need to…get him back…to the clinic."

"What say you climb up here an' ride whilst ye find yer breath?"

Miriam obeyed, and Ol' Mose gripped her arm as she climbed up onto the wagon seat beside him.

"Giddup there, Zeke. Move on, Zeb. We've got a man need's savin'." He slapped the reins and the pair of mules stepped into their harness in tandem.

They moved achingly slow, but Miriam used the time to fill her friend in on the highlights of their adventure.

"Alex only had one dose left of the medicine, so we've got to get Mr. Langley back to the clinic. Here…here's the turn." She motioned toward the opening in the trees. The branches and underbrush had grown up so much, she would have missed it had she not known where to look.

The grooves in Ol' Mose's brow creased more than usual as he turned the team off the road. "Miz Miriam, you've laid out quite a tale there. No wonder God's put ya close ta my mind these last couple hours. Had me prayin' fer ya hard, He did."

He reined in near where Alex hovered over the form of the large man by the mine opening. Miriam's heart clutched. Were they too late? She clambered down, biting back a cry when she landed on her bad leg.

A hacking cough sounded from the man on the ground, and it triggered a flood of relief through Miriam. He was still alive.

Alex stood, their eyes meeting across the distance. A world of emotions crossed between them. His relief. Courage. Fear. Love.

Alex took a step toward her. Another. Her own feet stepped forward, propelling her.

And then she was in his arms. He wrapped her tight as she clutched him. Breathing in his strength and love.

Alex loosened his grip too soon, but he slipped an arm around her waist as he turned to face Ol' Mose, who stood over Langley. "I just gave him another dose of elecampane. He'll need more within the hour, so we need to hurry."

"Can you walk, young feller?" Ol' Mose eyed Langley, who looked up at them through barely squinted eyes. Each breath rasped as it raised his chest.

"Yeah," the man wheezed, but he didn't make a move to rise.

Giving her side a final squeeze, Alex stepped away and squatted beside the man. "If you can get that side, Ol' Mose, let's lift him up."

Grunts sounded as they raised Langley between them and shuffled toward the wagon. Miriam limped ahead to take off the rear board so they could lay him in the back. The men propped Langley against several sacks of cornmeal.

"T'was out makin' deliveries to the mines." Ol' Mose said, motioning toward the half dozen crates stacked beside the bags.

"I'll sit back here with him." Alex hunkered down beside Langley.

Miriam's heart squeezed at the sight of her beloved. Even though this ne'er-do-well had kidnapped and tried to kill them, Alex did everything possible to save the man's life. How many other men would do the same? *Thank you, Lord, for bringing Alex to me.*

The ride to the clinic took forever.

Alex had Langley propped completely upright, but the coughs still shook his entire body. This cold air wasn't helping any, especially when the wind whipped up.

Bryan met them on the boardwalk in front of the clinic, a hand shading his eyes against the glare of the late afternoon sun. He didn't speak, but the question on his face was clear.

"This man's in a bad way. Help me get him in to a cot." Alex rose to his knees while he motioned to his brother.

Bryan obeyed, murmuring a greeting to Tad as they lifted him from the wagon. Miriam had already headed inside to get things ready.

"Reckon' I'll go get the sheriff if'n you youngsters have things in hand here," Ol' Mose said from his perch on the wagon.

Bryan's gaze jerked up to Alex. "The sheriff?"

Alex pinched his lips together as his mind skimmed

over what they'd been through. "Langley kidnapped Miriam, then marched us into an old mine at gunpoint. Set the place on fire and planned to kill all three of us. The smoke knocked him out first, though, so we were able to get out."

Bryan jerked upright. He looked like he would step back and leave Langley to fall in a heap.

"Come on, man. Help me get him inside." Alex nodded up the steps to the clinic door as he teetered under the weight of the giant.

Bryan's gaze skittered from the doorway where Miriam had disappeared, to Langley, then up to Alex. "This man tried to kill you and now you're saving his life?" Bryan didn't add "Have you gone daft?" but his tone said it for him.

"He's a human being, Bryan. My job is to help people. It's up to God and the law to judge them."

Eyes narrowing, Bryan studied him. Then a hint of a smile touched his mouth. "You finally figured that out, huh?"

A grin tugged at Alex's own mouth. "Sometimes it takes a good woman to point things out."

Bryan's brows shot up.

"Let's get him in." Alex spoke before his brother could, and stepped forward. Bryan didn't have a choice but to do the same.

For once, it was a good thing his brother knew how to hold his tongue.

Alex pushed his horse into a jog as the mountain trail leveled out. According to Miriam's directions, he shouldn't be far now. She'd certainly been right about it taking almost half a day to maneuver the mountain trails to the Bryant Ranch.

A dog barked in the distance. He must be close. A side road split off from the main wagon path he traveled, and Alex took the smaller fork left. The trees opened to a clearing, where a log cabin first caught his eye. Its structure was simple, with a railed porch spanning the front. White curtains hung in the windows, and rocks outlined a few barren shrubs in front of the porch. Would those spindly plants produce flowers in the spring?

To the left stood the barn, with fences fanning out on three sides. One of the large double doors opened, and out frisked a mid-sized dog. It glanced back inside the door and barked as Gideon emerged.

Alex's chest tightened at the sight of the man he'd come to see. Surely Gideon wouldn't be angry at his news. Would he?

When Gideon saw him, his face broke into a grin and his wide steps veered from the path to the house as he approached Alex.

Alex dismounted and stepped forward to shake the man's hand.

"Donaghue. Good to see you." And then Gideon's face clouded as his grip tightened. "Where's Miriam? What's wrong?"

Alex held up his other hand to stop the barrage. "She's fine. Sends her love to you and Mrs. Bryant. I just stopped by to discuss something with you."

Gideon relaxed and stepped back as Alex gazed around the clearing. "Nice place you have here." He turned back to Gideon with a grin. "It's peaceful."

"That's what we like about it." Gideon reached for the

reins. "Come inside while I put your horse away. Leah'll have something good to feed you."

That didn't sound like a bad offer, so Alex followed Gideon toward the front steps where the man let loose a whistle, then waited expectantly. Gideon's profile favored Miriam's. Her features were softer, and her coloring more fair, but they had the same strong jaw and chin. The same tip at the end of their nose. The same wide eyes. His chest ached as he thought of her.

Leah Bryant appeared on the front porch, wiping her hands on her apron. Her face brightened when she saw him. "You brought Miriam home?" Her gaze flitted over the horse, then drifted around the yard. "Where is she?"

He felt like a heel. "Sorry, ma'am. She said she had too many things to take care of in town. And I wasn't sure her knee was ready for so many hours on horseback to get up here. She sends her love though."

Mrs. Bryant worked hard to cover her disappointment. "Well, please come in Doctor Donaghue." Her southern accent crept out as she stepped to the side and held the door for him. "I was just taking sweet rolls out of the oven, and I have coffee warm. You couldn't have come at a better time."

The three of them chatted in amiable conversation over coffee and cinnamon rolls that melted on his tongue. Gideon was a bit reserved, occasionally eyeing him, as Alex answered one of Mrs. Bryant's questions. The man was plainly curious about his business here, but he didn't seem hostile. Had Alex expected him to be? Still, Alex's palms were damp as he drained the last sip of his coffee—and not just from the heat of the mug.

"I have a mare in the barn that should be foaling soon. Care to have a look at her, Doc?" Gideon leaned back in his chair, watching Alex.

Alex met the man's gaze. "Be happy to."

They strode along the well-worn path to the barn. Alex clenched and unclenched his fists as he tried to find a way to raise his question. The inside of the barn was dark, and Alex blinked as his eyes adjusted to the dimness.

A mare nickered to them, and Gideon met her at the stall door, taking her large head in his hands as he crooned. "Howdy, girl. You feelin' okay today? Brought the doc to see how close you are."

Alex slipped into the stall, and ran his hands down the mare's neck, over her distended abdomen, and across her hindquarters. He bent down to peer at her udder, then eased his hand under to feel of its firmness. A drop of white milk appeared on the tip when he touched it. Lastly, he raised the mare's tail and eyed the loosening of the muscles underneath. He turned to Gideon, resting a hand on the horse's back. "Gideon, to be honest, you've probably seen more pregnant mares than I have. She looks close to me. Today or tomorrow."

The other man nodded, approval reflected in his eyes. Was it because of his diagnosis? Or the fact that he'd been honest about his experience not equaling Gideon's?

Alex let himself out of the stall and draped an arm over a rail as Gideon continued to stroke the mare. Now was the time.

He cleared his throat. "I, um, would like to ask you something."

Gideon didn't answer. Didn't turn, just kept running his hands down the horse's jaw as she dozed. He wasn't making this easy.

"I'd like to marry your sister, Gideon. I'd like your blessing, if you're willing to give it." There. It was out. But he couldn't take a breath as he watched Miriam's older brother.

The man's gaze rose to somewhere in the distance. Farther than the stall wall where his eyes landed. His expression was impossible to read. Finally he spoke a single word. "Why?"

Alex swallowed. No, not making this easy. "Because I love her. She's the most amazing woman I've ever met." How did he put into words how he felt about Miriam? Especially to her brother.

Gideon nodded, then stood quiet for another moment. At last he sighed. "It's all right with me." He turned to look at Alex dead-on. "But the final decision is Miriam's."

Relief coursed through Alex. He wanted to let out a whoop, but settled for a grin. "Thank you." Reaching into his coat pocket, Alex pulled out a paper, folded and sealed. "Miriam said I had to wait until after I asked to give you this."

Gideon raised a brow, but took the paper, split the wax seal, and started reading.

Alex licked his lips as he eyed the man, but it was like watching an expert cardsharp. No facial expression except for a single raised brow, before he refolded the paper and slipped it into his pocket.

After a final pat on the mare's neck, Gideon turned to Alex and rested a hand on his shoulder. "I reckon' it's settled then. Let's go tell Leah the good news."

Chapter Twenty-Seven

"Did they say when they're coming down for the wedding?" Miriam tugged Alex's arm as they strolled on the road skirting the edge of town.

Alex had returned from Gideon and Leah's late last night, and he'd left Bryan in the clinic again today while Alex saw to "business" around town. Now evening had come and the clinic was closed, so she'd finally stolen him away to hear the details of his conversation with her brother.

"Two weeks. He tried to convince me to wait until spring, but I held my ground." Alex shot her a grin that warmed all the way to her toes.

"Two weeks is good." She turned her face up to absorb the last few rays of the setting sun.

They walked in silence for several minutes, until Alex spoke. "I talked to the sheriff today."

She jerked her gaze to him. "What'd he say?"

"Wanted to move Langley to a cell. I told him he needed to stay at the clinic for a couple more days at least."

She studied his expression. Having the man there where she worked still sent a tingle of unease down her spine. But he was so sick, barely strong enough to feed himself. They couldn't send him away just yet. And Bryan had taken over the man's care completely, so she didn't have to spend time around him.

Alex stopped walking and searched her eyes. "Would you rather I have him moved to the jail?"

She forced her face into a smile, but it wasn't so hard. "No. He's where he needs to be."

The line of his mouth eased. "You're amazing."

Miriam couldn't hold his gaze as warmth crept up her neck. "Did the sheriff say what he'd do with Mr. Langley when he's better?"

"He's working on an idea. I thought it a good one myself."

She raised her brows.

"Since Langley's mental state is...questionable, he thought it best the man leaves this part of the territory. He's sending him back to Kansas. That's where the brothers hail from, and apparently Tad still has family there. The local sheriff there has a work program for his long term inmates, to make them into responsible citizens."

Relief sank through her, relaxing the muscles in her shoulders and neck. "That sounds like a great plan. Do you think he'll be well enough to work?"

"I asked the sheriff to make sure he'll be under the care of a physician in Kansas."

Warmth washed through her chest as she stared into Alex's eyes. "You're a good man, Alex Donaghue. The best."

He looked away, red seeping into his cheeks. He started walking again.

They strolled for several minutes, passing the edge of town on their left and tall grass on their right, as the hills prepared to give way to the mountains. The church yard appeared up ahead. Even though they hadn't had a preacher for over a year, someone still tended the building and the rose vines crawling along the fence. Would they ever have a pastor again? How wonderful it would be to join with other Christians each week, and study the Scripture under the direction of a man called by God.

"You know, you never answered my question."

Miriam's gaze found Alex again and searched his face. "Which question was that?"

"Where you want to live. I promised you could decide, m'lady. Boston? New York? Paris?"

He shot her a smile. The corners of his mouth tipped, but the grin didn't light his eyes like usual. Instead, there were tiny creases at the outside corners where his lashes met. Did he really think she wanted to be anywhere other than here? Working alongside him to make a difference in other people's lives.

She stopped walking, and Alex paused, turning toward her. His jaw tightened, and his face lost all hint of a smile. "M'lady?"

"Alex, it matters not to me where we go. I'd just as soon stay here, as long as we can keep helping these people."

His brow puckered. "Stay here? But you want to travel. I'll need to settle down and work somewhere, but I have a little money saved to get us there."

She raised her hand to smooth the wrinkle in his brow. "I used to think I wanted that. But I finally realized that I hadn't given that part to God. Hadn't asked Him to show me exactly what He has planned for me. And when I finally put my future in God's hands, you know what I discovered?" She removed her hand from the crook of his arm, and lifted both his hands to her waist. Alex's arms moved reluctantly, as if he were trying to distance himself. Afraid of what she would say?

"What?" He finally met her gaze and tightened his arms around her. His eyes read uncertainty. But there was resolve there too.

Miriam's heart swelled. Would he leave this place where he'd established himself, just to make her happy? How did she deserve this man? *Thank You, Lord. Your ways truly are higher than mine.*

Slipping her hands around his neck, she smiled. "I realized God had something better planned for me all along. It's not seeing new sights that will make me happy, it's finding His plan for me. Finding my purpose. What He created me to do."

Alex's eyes widened, a tiny spark igniting them. "And what's that?"

"Working with you. Helping these people. Making a difference, no matter how small. Being His tool."

A myriad of emotions played across Alex's face. So much that he seemed to struggle to contain them all. His grip tightened at her waist, and he lowered his forehead to rest on hers. His breathing grew labored, and the tickle of its warmth caressed her skin. "You can't imagine how happy that makes me. It won't be easy. I can't promise it will. But I can promise I'll love and cherish you with every ounce of my being."

She fingered the thick hair at the nape of his neck, as moisture clogged her throat. "That's more than I ever dreamed of."

Her eyes drifted closed as his mouth claimed hers.

"Shall we head to the church?"

Eyeing herself in the mirror of her room at the boarding house, Miriam twisted a curl falling around her face. It still wouldn't lay right. But better this time. Stepping back, she pressed her hands down the front of her skirt.

"You're beautiful, Miri. The loveliest bride I've ever seen."

She turned to Leah, nibbling her lip as she tried for a smile. "Do you think I look all right?"

Leah's eyes shimmered as she took Miriam's hands and held them out. Her gaze roamed from Miriam's hair all the way down to the hem of her pale blue muslin gown. "You're amazing. So beautiful it makes me want to cry."

A rush of moisture stung Miriam's own eyes, and she stepped forward into Leah's arms. "Thank you."

Leah clutched her tight, and Miriam squeezed her eyes against the rush of emotion churning in her. "Thank you for everything."

Leah finally pulled back, gripping Miriam's upper arms. "I'm only going to say this once, because neither one of us should walk into your wedding all red and puffy-eyed. I'm so happy for you, Miriam. I have total peace that Alex is the man God has planned for you. But I'm going to miss you more than I can say. Please don't be a stranger."

Miriam sniffed, but it didn't stop the moisture filling her eyes. "I love you, too. I'm sorry I won't be able to go with you on our trip this summer. But my place is here."

Squeezing her hand, a funny look came into Leah's eyes, and her mouth spread into a grin that lit every part of her face. "Of course it is. But I may have needed to back out of the trip anyway."

Miriam raised a brow. Was Leah…?

Her friend's pretty white teeth flashed as she giggled. Her hand crept to her midsection. "Gideon and I have good news."

Miriam squealed and pulled Leah into a tight hug. "Oh, that's wonderful! Oh, Leah, I'm so happy for you." More tears stung as Leah clutched her tight and they both laughed and chattered.

"When will it come?"

"Doc Bryan says May, most likely."

Stepping back, Miriam eyed her. "Bryan knows about it before me?"

Leah shrugged. "He's the doctor. We've been hoping..." Her cheeks bloomed pink and she dropped her gaze. "I mean it's been so long."

Miriam couldn't help a chuckle. She'd wondered more than once why two years had passed since Gideon and Leah's marriage, without any sign of Leah's being "in the family way."

"Well I'm so happy for you I could burst." Miriam took Leah's hand and turned toward the door. "That's exactly the news to make my wedding day perfect."

Leah gasped, tightening her grip on Miriam's hand. "Your wedding. We have to get you to the church."

Alex shuffled from one foot to the other as he stood in the front of the church. What was taking so long?

A chuckle drifted from Bryan, who stood beside him. "She's coming, man. Relax."

Of course she was coming. Alex adjusted the string tie at his neck. Right? Miriam wouldn't back out now. He scanned the crowd. It was amazing how many people had come for their little ceremony. So many of their patients. The sight sent a warmth through his chest. Ol' Mose sat in the second row beside Mrs. Malmgren. The old freighter had his hair slicked to the side, and a grin split his face like a proud tom cat. What was going on between those two?

The back door opened, grabbing his attention and tightening every muscle in him. Leah Bryant slipped through, a smile lighting her face as she stepped down the aisle and stopped across from him. She gave him a secretive grin.

Anticipation tightened his stomach as he focused his attention on the back door. Miriam had to be next, right?

At last, the wood hinge creaked as the door opened. Gideon was the first over the threshold, and on his arm walked a woman so beautiful she took his breath away. Miriam's hair was coiled high, revealing the slender grace of her neck. A few loose curls hung down, framing her heart-shaped face. Her lips formed a gentle smile. Even now, his own mouth remembered their taste and feel.

As she strolled toward him, Alex's eyes roamed up to hers. His breath caught. The love in her gaze. The devotion. The purity. It flooded his soul, swelling his heart to overflowing. *Lord, help me deserve her.*

A peace washed through him. Yes, with God's help. He would love this woman with every fiber of his being.

As Miriam reached the front of the church on her brother's arm, Alex was barely aware of the judge speaking beside him.

"Who gives this woman in marriage?"

"My wife and I do." Gideon's deep voice rumbled the words as he shot a glance at Leah on Miriam's other side.

Miriam reached up to kiss her brother on the cheek, murmuring something in his ear. He smiled into her face, then glanced up at Alex. For a moment, their gazes locked. It was the transfer. Gideon was entrusting one of his most precious possessions—his sister. Alex accepted the offer, the gift. The treasure.

As Alex received Miriam's hand, his gaze drifted down to his bride. How could she be more amazing? Radiant. He brought her fingers up and pressed a kiss on her knuckles.

They turned together to face the judge, and Alex squeezed her hand. Miriam's responding pressure sent another surge of gratitude through his chest. *With Your help, Lord.*

Did you enjoy this book? I hope so!

Would you take a quick minute to leave a review?
http://www.amazon.com/dp/B00T8XN9Q2/

It doesn't have to be long. Just a sentence or two telling what you liked about the book!

About the Author

Misty M. Beller writes romantic mountain stories, set in the 1800s and woven with the message of God's love.

She was raised on a farm in South Carolina, so her Southern roots run deep. Growing up, her family was close, and they continue to keep that priority today. Her husband and children now add another dimension to her life, keeping her both grounded and crazy.

God has placed a desire in Misty's heart to combine her love for Christian fiction and the simpler ranch life, writing historical novels that display God's abundant love through the twists and turns in the lives of her characters.

Sign up for e-mail updates when future books are available!
www.MistyMBeller.com

Don't miss the other books by
Misty M. Beller

The Mountain Series
The Lady and the Mountain Man
The Lady and the Mountain Doctor
The Lady and the Mountain Fire
The Lady and the Mountain Promise
The Lady and the Mountain Call
This Treacherous Journey
This Wilderness Journey
This Freedom Journey (novella)
This Courageous Journey
This Homeward Journey
This Daring Journey
This Healing Journey

Texas Rancher Trilogy
The Rancher Takes a Cook
The Ranger Takes a Bride
The Rancher Takes a Cowgirl

Wyoming Mountain Tales
A Pony Express Romance
A Rocky Mountain Romance
A Sweetwater River Romance
A Mountain Christmas Romance

Hearts of Montana
Hope's Highest Mountain
Love's Mountain Quest
Faith's Mountain Home

Call of the Rockies
Freedom in the Mountain Wind
Hope in the Mountain River
Light in the Mountain Sky